ADVENTURES ON THE GO

ADVENTURES ON THE GO

Adventures on the Go

FALL, 2021

VOLUME 1 **BOOK 1**

COPYRIGHT©2021, OFFBEAT PUBLISHING

ISBN: 978-1-950464-01-2 (PAPERBACK)
ISBN: 978-1-950464-02-9 (EBOOK)

Special THANKS to: Michael Gehlert of Aschaffenburg, Germany, for the use of his likeness for The Journal of Eye Collector D.R. Melvin.

ATTENTION WRITERS, WE ARE ACCEPTING WELL-WRITTEN SHORT STORY SUBMISSIONS FOR CONSIDERATION IN FUTURE BOOKS. FOR MORE, VISIT:
WWW.OFFBEATREADS.COM/ABOUTANDCONTACT

letters to the editor:
OffBeatReads@pm.me
Put *Letter to Editor* in Subject.
Email content subject to publication in future *Adventures on the Go.*

WWW.OFFBEATREADS.COM

EDITOR'S NOTE

WITH MUCH EXCITEMENT I introduce you to Book 1 of *Adventures on the Go*; a small, affordable, appealing offering intended to be carried with you wherever you go.

For a while now, OffBeatReads has sought out ways to fill a void in today's literary culture. Society seems broken down into two main categories. Some love to read, some do not. Obvious, right? As avid readers ourselves, we asked what kind of book we would like to see available, and what has the greatest chance of reaching not only readers, but people who would naturally default to watching a movie or playing video games instead. The idea needed to be original as possible, inexpensive, and easy to take along in a pocket, handbag, or the like.

We've always adored pulp magazines from the early to mid 1900s like *Planet Stories, Famous Fantastic Mysteries, Strange Tales,* and others. "Maybe we could do something a little like that," I said, gazing at the few collector's rags we have on our office shelves. We cherish those—and they take my mind back. I imagine it happened like this... New York... maybe Chicago... our well-known private eye enters the office and throws his fedora on my desk. He looks at my writing partner:

"Help me off with my coat pretty lady. I practically got skinned by Lewis Kreger and his boys."

I gasp. "You shot?"

"Just skinned."

He plops down on the sofa and lights one with the charisma and charm earned with his battle scars. Then he breathes a heavy sigh of weariness and takes a sniff of the air.

"I don't smell any food. We eatin' dinner?"

My partner and I look at each other. It's nearly midnight.

"Uh, we can scrounge something up. What'll you have?"

"Bourbon."

And we knew how he liked it. A double, neat.

Like all the times before, we associated the aroma of woodsy alcohol with our brave gumshoe falling asleep. We didn't have long to talk. I opened my mouth but he beat me to the punch.

"What you two up to?"

"We were trying to drum up an idea for a series of books."

He twisted his stiff and beaten body into a more tolerable position, threw down the last swallow of bourbon, and tossed his cigarette into the tumbler.

"Do a pulp."

Now, I'm not sure how original this tiny book is, and I'm not sure what to call it, but we hope it will reinforce a love of stories for you, and that it will reach those who may not normally give an adventure a try. You can expect new, original stories, and others that may ring familiar and even the not so well-known, yet intriguing tales.

Seriously speaking, some stories may seem improper or even downright wrong to you, especially in today's culture. Know that we will never be provocative just to be provocative, and never offend just to offend. And—we will also *never* advocate hate nor discrimination or ANY kind. This said, each work we present should be judged with knowledge of the era and context in which it was written. We are trusting you to be a discerning reader who understands this, and knows that reading can have effects beyond "feel-good entertainment". There may be something nostalgic, something to learn, or something to never forget.

HAVE AN ADVENTURE!

Robert Kimbrell

ROBERT KIMBRELL, EDITOR

The Journal of Eye Collector D.R. Melvin

Written by

Robert Kimbrell

To whom this may concern,

The release of this journal makes you privy to the disturbing mind of Dylan R. Melvin. One would think a story such as this would make for sensational headlines, but for whatever reason, the serial killer of Jackson County was widely under-reported.

The first victim's body was found with both eyes removed *before* her murder. Due to this strange fact, bureau resources worked in tandem with local law enforcement from the start to make an apprehension as quickly as possible.

As you will see, although the man convicted of these crimes had extreme issues, he was clever and intelligent. His methods and madness were contrived from a deeply troubled place. It is indeed sad that this man did not seek nor receive the mental help he needed. Regardless, any sympathy for Dylan Melvin should not overshadow the horrors experienced by his victims.

If I have any misgivings as to our handling of this case at the time, it is that we did not conclude that the disappearances were the work of this man earlier in the investigation.

Lastly, in full disclosure, there were twelve rather small sections of Melvin's writings that were too extreme, violent, or gruesome for publishing. It was my sole decision to remove these sections entirely. Beyond that, the story is unaffected, and everything you are about to read is unaltered and completely unchanged.

Yours,
Agent Mareno

Dear Investigators,

I am not a proud man. I am flawed as much as anyone else and far beyond repentance. So that law enforcement and the media will know the truth, I decided to write events as I see them. As dark as it may seem to you, the world needs to know my legacy. Right or wrong, beautiful or ugly, my legacy is all I have. Let these writings also serve as my full and legal confession. I will have nothing more to say on these matters; not in a court of law, not ever.

Yours,
D.R. Melvin

MY FIRST LOVE was Kim. I'm going way back to when I was a wee kid, five years of age. Her family lived caddy-cornered across the street from our house, and we went to the same elementary school together. Her brown hair with a cute boyish cut, brown eyes to match and adorable dimples melted me. What I felt for her could have been infatuation or a childish crush. Still, I cared for her more than anything or anyone else. But, I was a nerdy greaseball kid in a lower-middle-class family. Kim didn't take an interest in me whatsoever. No girl did.

There are other things about my childhood I'll share with you, but when you consider everything, it all boiled down to me being a nerdy reject. It took me many years to figure out how to deal with the overwhelming world. I could be by myself, in essence be a passive recluse with my life, or I could put on my mask of societal norms and dive into public waters.

This doesn't make me crazy. Aren't you a lot like this?

People point to their chest when speaking of the heart, or talk of the soul as if it's some tangible thing somewhere inside. No. When I think of Kim, when I think of the others, I can tell you where the heart resides. I can tell you where the soul is...

> *There is no secret way*
> *to decipher what you're seeing*
> *and no sincerity elsewhere—*
> *no essence of her being.*
> *Only gaze into her soul,*
> *for truth without the lies.*
> *There's no other way to know her*
> *but in the colors of her eyes.*

EVEN AT AGE six I knew something set me apart from my peers. Something was different. Every step in public was filled with dread, fear. Were my actions good or bad? Was I going to be made fun of? Was I going to mess up? Not viewing myself as an equal to others, I questioned incessantly what could be wrong with me. However, I also felt that how I viewed people and events was unique and special in some way. If only I could be set free, I had something profound to offer the world.

Throughout the teen years, these feelings remained with me. Anxiety held on fast, the contrast between me and everyone else grew. It seemed I would never fit in and never find a comfortable normal, let alone success in some form.

Afraid of uncontrollably tripping into a mental quicksand and becoming some type of monster, I chose to force myself into situations that involved human interactions. Looking back, it was self-imposed exposure therapy. If I could not be normal, perhaps I could act normal enough. When that failed, as I suspected it would, I became silly just to magnify my alien self. Yes, I was still laughed at and picked on, but at least I earned it with my actions. Being an outcast didn't feel abnormal.

After my Father reluctantly allowed me to get a part-time job during my senior year of high school, I afforded a new haircut and decent clothes. I then slipped on a helping of pretend confidence, and ditched the silliness. All that helped me fit in just enough that for small chunks of time I could more or less deal with the pressures of my existence. Lying to myself, I said, "You are different but in a *good* way. You're okay!" At least I was able to go to work, run errands; *appear* normal. After awhile I even bought a used truck with my saved minimum wage earnings.

As far as my Father goes, he was the beast that caged me. Even when his health deteriorated I was the focus of his anger and crushing over-protective thumb. For now, let that point stew. There will be more about him later.

You surely find this boring by now. Where is the drama? The tragedy? The horror?

Whether you believe it or not, we all seek horror. Horror allows us to respond with our self-righteous display of ugliness-shunning before we turn a blind eye to it. We feel better about ourselves and escape responsibility. Only action can precipitate change, but posturing do-gooders only resort to gossiping and bitching about how terrible the thing is. These types are the real despicable ones.

So let's talk about Rebecca. She was the first addition to my collection. During my super brief stint with her, I finished transforming into the monster I had been trying to put off. She was in danger and there was nothing I could do about it.

REBECCA

O NE PARTICULAR DAY in early spring, a gray drizzle of rain comple-mented my ruthless bout of anxiety and paranoia. The real and overwhelming thought continued to strike at me that I could sink so low I'd never be able to rebound. So I drove to a small but well-known hole-in-the-wall bar named Wine and Dines. (It's still there today, but goes by a different name.) I parked and strolled apprehensively to its maroon awning which sat directly under the cast of a streetlamp on the corner of Cherry and Lake streets.

The door flicked the antique bell hanging on a thin strip of curled metal. Expressionless, several people at the end of the bar turned to see who had entered. Now the center of attention, my nervousness grew, until my eyes met those of one woman in particular. When everyone else turned their heads away, hers remained.

A woman with her kind of beauty had never looked at me for more than a second, that is unless she was taking in how ridiculous I appeared or sensing my frail character. As I searched for the right seat that would allow me to have my back against the wall, her glances shifted between me and her drink. I was beginning to feel like that frightened little boy all over again. For a Moment, I wondered how it felt to have a true and com-plete mental flip out. For years I had wondered... when one went crazy, did it happen suddenly, without conscious awareness of it? Did going crazy mean a switch flipped somewhere in the brain but one *did* have full conscious awareness of it? And, if it happened to me and I was aware I had gone crazy, would I involuntarily act out whatever my crazy part wanted me to?

Back to the bar.

Perhaps she was still looking my way because I looked stupid with my red button-up shirt and gray wool overcoat... maybe my hair was messed up. Whatever the reason for her glances, I dared not return them for fear of inviting attention that I wasn't mentally equipped to handle. When I spotted a table in the distance that required me to pass by her, I gave a half-smile,

enough to be friendly, then lowered my head and took my first step. Looking away or lowering my head was the habitual way my lack of confidence chose to reveal itself.

Mustering a stride of nonchalance, I traced the imaginary dotted line toward my chosen table. *Trying to be normal.* A sudden spark of fear threatened to spoil everything, but I propped my chin up with all the courage I could.

"Need a seat? This one's open."

My Momentum stopped. I stared at her for several seconds not knowing what to say. "I'm sorry?"

She kept the same smile. "I said, this seat is open."

My clumsy nod thanked her as I connected with the stool like a magnet. I didn't want to sit there but didn't have any idea how to tell her no. Now I would have people walking behind me and be forced to interact. No control over the space around me.

Rebecca began the small talk. Another voice interrupted.

"I'm not letting go of you!"

So audible was he that I almost turned to see the source, then I realized. D.R.—people called me D.R. when I was young—was speaking to me. So much time and effort trying to leave him behind, yet that damn annoying reject, that *brat*, introduced himself. How could that be? Oddly and quickly though, my anger vanished. Some bit of my soul calmed as if I had been waiting on him to return as an old buddy or the prodigal's son.

"I'm always gonna be here for you, Dylan."

Trying to not make a fool of myself in the presence of the woman, I directed words at him with my brain hoping he could hear them. *Leave me alone right now* I told him.

Something was seriously wrong with me. Hearing voices! Yet, I could see him in my mind's eye, feel him too—another *me* within *me*. His following silence prompted my guilt. I shouldn't have yelled at him like that.

"Are you alright?"

"Sorry. Battle weary I guess." What the hell does that mean? "Dealing with some things," I added. "Don't let me interrupt your evening."

She looked perturbed. "Stop apologizing. What you drinking?"

At this Moment the bartender, a burly but nice-natured guy, leaned on his towel in front of us and waited for my answer.

"Vodka. A double, neat… whatever's in the well."

Her perturbed look dissipated when she witnessed the possibility that I wasn't a total moron. So I could order my own drink. Woohoo. Initially, I felt pride at how confident I was apparently becoming. But I remembered, fools can get lucky, and luck isn't good enough. Luck doesn't keep the girl around. On top of that, I should have chosen a top-shelf brand— shown better self-worth.

And the young brat was gone. His absence was palpable as his presence. He'd be back.

We went on making mostly small talk for about ten minutes when she mentioned how surprised she was that I hadn't been hitting on her.

"Refreshing," she said. "I'm Rebecca."

Realizing I was a dumb ass for not introducing myself, I reached to shake her hand. "Dylan."

For the next half hour she went on to share things of a personal nature with me like where she worked, the neighborhood where she lived, and details about her family. Not street smart. There are some real weirdos in the world.

And no, it's not like I was *planning* on taking advantage of her or hurting her in any way. There was the moment at the end, after I paid for my drinks and got up to leave. She wrote her number on a napkin and handed it to me. Nothing like that had ever happened to me.

It was then that I saw straight into her gorgeous golden brown eyes. The blackness of her pupils were filled with amazing sparks and curved lights. What a woman! I would never be worthy of the likes of her. Maybe if I was lucky, for a night, but something meaningful? A relationship of depth where I could ever be me without being a reject? No. I knew then like I always knew, I was different. No woman would value me.

A buildup of fuming anger rose inside me. I tried to quell it; make my escape as a nice guy and get out of that bar. *Just get out!* Surely my difficult smile appeared stern to her as I said goodbye and exited.

The anxiety, the burdens, the guilt—all of it—boiled inside me.

I wanted her or somebody deeply as a partner and lover but I was a worthless mistake of an adult that didn't know his way in the world. Merely touching her hand during the overly formal handshake was amazing. Inhaling deeply, I breathed into my lungs the resignation that I'd end the night feeling like the failure I am. If I did call her, she'd find a reason to gradually stop communicating with me. Any possibility of something meaningful with her would end in me not being good enough or me getting hurt.

It wasn't going to be. Not this time. Not ever again.

MY WIFE
AND THE UNGODLY

JUDGING BY HOW I acted with Rebecca, you'll be surprised to know I was married to a gal named Monica. Until she physically let herself go, she was only a slightly overweight girl with a super nice, round backside. Perfect actually.

I was twenty, she was eighteen, still in high school. And yes, her parents were against me from the start. Having graduated two years prior, I was too old and not the type of rugged cowboy type they desired for her. Monica's Mother soon came to graciously accept me because at that time I was a churchgoer (I attended a non-denominational church because it's what Dad made me do), and treated Monica with utmost kindness and respect. Apparently, she assumed there was hope. Her Father was an egotistical, spoiled ass who had every toy he wanted in the barn, and he loved to act like an all-wise god. With him there was one way only in which to see and do things.

What I had going for me was the fact that Monica was young and naive... and so for some odd reason, she was enamored with me. It could have been that I was the first in her life that shamelessly threw myself at her. So she had no doubts about how I felt. Monica also wanted a "good Christian man" to marry. Beyond those reasons, I looked nothing like her Father and definitely didn't act like him. Maybe the fact that I was different was a positive in her mind.

After gaining her trust, then pressuring her, we had sex—premarital sex. Oh, she felt SO guilty. But in her eyes, the only thing worse than premarital sex was not marrying the one she had sex with. She had to make things right by tying the knot.

After only two years we divorced. Of course, living together had magnified our fundamental differences. But she didn't believe in divorce. That is, not until it became inconvenient for her to love me. According to her, I only wanted sex. Not true, but isn't *sex* something married couples do?

Against her will, I got what I wanted. She bitched and whined about how traumatic it was.

"If you just get out I won't speak of it. Just get out!"

And those self-proclaimed Christians of the church that had all professed and acted like I was a valued member of the family, ignored me when news of the divorce spread. The hypocrites were masters at expounding their virtues until "loving a sinner" became inconvenient and unpopular for them. My soul was suddenly not worth saving.

Let's see, I turned twenty-one before I had sex with her, and it was my first time too. Imagine, being a young man, twenty-one years old, and still being a virgin. Sure, it can be admirable when a young person has the goal of abstinence, but I didn't care about that. Everything must consider it's context, and my context was formed early on...

THE DARKNESS OF
MY CHILDHOOD

How did I get so messed up? Looking back I see and admit that things were disturbed.

As I said earlier, I was twenty-one when I had sex for the first time. You want to know when I committed my first act of violence? Ten.

We lived three blocks away from the town square, on the corner of Mulberry and Simpson. Our house was one of the first in the area when people began settling there over two hundred years ago. Unfortunately, any historic value was lost over time due to various remodels and repairs, and new construction on the east end of town made our section unpopular. Our small one car garage ran alongside a narrow alley that split our block in half. On the other side of that alley, a large yard, then a house. On the other side of our house, around the corner that is, was an ugly unmaintained stucco made into two apartments. Across the street, three homes faced ours as if seating an audience for our dysfunctional family show. Nothing would conceal our stage play from neighbors. My Father, my life, my tears, Mom's shame—it was all a spectacle.

Late one evening, Dad was upset. No, he hadn't been drinking alcohol. He only drank from his own internal rage. Curled up in a deep sleep in my bedroom, I sat straight up. Dad was yelling furiously from the kitchen. "You need to fill the goddamn ice. It's the middle of summer you sonofabitch!". Mom replied with words he didn't find acceptable, and that's when he threw the plastic ice cube trays at her along with more hateful words.

Everyone else's Father seemed so gentle and mature compared to mine.

I quietly pushed the side screen door open and ran to the other side of the garage next to the alley. It didn't matter who saw me, I just needed space between me and the ugliness.

In my light blue flannel pajamas, I squatted on a small patch of grass, cupped my face to my hands, and cried. Not caring if the neighbors heard me, I wailed. At any Moment Dad could appear, grab me by the neck and drag me back to the house for a whipping. I wanted him dead so the hurt would stop. That would make the world better. Just gone.

Movement at the corner of my eye caused me to flinch. *Oh no* I thought... *he's gonna get me!*

A scared-stiff whimper of expectation squeezed from my lips as I pressed shut my eyes. No hand grabbed me. I peeked through my eyelids to see a bushy squirrel's tail jarting up and down. It was busy digging at the grass behind our two metal trash cans.

Something suddenly exploded to the surface from within. It was some sort of rage, a crazed spilling of all my emotions. My face grew hot, my vision blurred, my skin tingled. I had gone to that spot to be safe, how dare this stupid animal scare me there. Unusually afraid of nothing, I honed in on the tail.

Because I was somewhat outside myself at the time, my memory is a little hazy. I do remember leaping headfirst and grabbing the tail... the squirrel was flailing and scratching at my arm while I held it in the air. Standing, raging, I swung it into the corner of the garage. It tried to curl back to counter-attack and break free but I wouldn't let it. I swung it again... and again... and again... into the garage. It let out high-pitched screeches that I still hear to this day.

When done, I stood for quite some time, still holding the warm bag of squished organs by the tail... sweating... breathing fast... laughing and crying with satisfaction. The red blood and fur mixture stuck to the white paint is something Dad would see tomorrow. And he would ask me if I knew anything about it. Didn't matter though. I was alive, *really* alive for the first time and I knew it! Until that Moment I'd felt like a mere observer of life. I had been moving about from one scene to the next, disconnected and numb, tolerating everything around me—never an actual participant in events.

Without spotting me, Dad backed out of the driveway and drove off. Maybe he went to another woman's house. Didn't matter. *I was at peace.* I wanted to feel it all again.

A short while ago I was cleaning and polishing my 440 stainless steel tool of choice: the enucleation spoon. It is a long-handled surgical tool with a triangular notch in the bowl. If I fashioned a thicker handle, out of wood perhaps, it would be easier to twist with my wrist behind the eye to extract it. It's pretty the way it is though, and wearing one of those long rubber cleaning gloves provides ample grip enough.

The first trick is working around the eyelid properly in order to avoid damaging the eyeball. After that, one must sever the muscles without damaging the eyeball using the sharpened notch in the spoon. I made a rookie mistake on the first attempt, messing up Rebecca's eye using a normal kitchen spoon. I felt bad about that, still do. The longer handle and notch makes all the difference. So when I researched and found the correct tool for the job, I ordered one. Yes, I kept her body a few days until I was able to properly scoop out her other eye.

Technically (insert laughter here), the "trick" is making sure the woman is unable to move. It is a given that if she puts up a fight or squirms it should be dealt with before the sacred extraction.

You will call me crazy, insane, maybe call me a psychopath, but I don't think I am. I manage to think clearly, methodically, even knowing all the while that what I'm doing is immoral. How do I excuse what I've done? I do not excuse my actions. I am different because my life circumstances made me so, and what I do is the result of it all. The world will not grant the special ones a license, therefore I grant one to myself.

Oh yes. After dropping the squirrel where I stood, I ran inside to wash my hands, change into my other pajamas and join Mom in the living room. I was way too young to absorb her entire outpouring of emotions, but I sympathized (while inwardly celebrating my victory over another life) as much as I could. She held me and sobbed for what must've been an hour while I sat on her lap consoling her, tapping along each ivory-colored pearl of her necklace. It was the only thing she owned with any real value.

Mom never did say anything about finding my pajamas in the hamper.

FIRST REAL DATE
WITH REBECCA

W HEN ONE IS trying to deceive another there are times you have to take control of the pretense by offering it. For instance, "I'm doing this because of this" or, more specifically, "Oh yes, I got this shipment of formaldehyde delivered here for my friend... he's learning criminal justice..." blah blah...

Most of the time, however, I have found it easier to carry a demeanor of humility and let illusion simply unfold. Must be ready to answer without stuttering though.

"What do you do?" Rebecca inquired. And the night was on its way to unfolding.

I recalled our talk at the bar where I already answered that question. Maybe she is testing me.

"Computer Analyst."

Three nights prior I had called her, asking her to my quaint farmhouse for a quiet evening after a long work week. "No pressure at all," I told her. "Never pressure. We can always meet somewhere in public if you want, but thought I'd open up my house. We can relax and have good conversation."

With little to no hesitation, she agreed. She even offered to pick up pizza on the way over.

When she arrived it was rather funny. While stealing glances of the décor and arrangement of my furniture, she continued the conversation as if we never had a pause of three days in the middle.

"What does a computer analyst do?"

"This one analyzes mostly numbers relating to sales." I gave a faint partial laugh. "Please don't make me talk about it. Long week as usual. Make good money though. You said you're a paralegal?"

She nodded. "For Long, Peeler, and Ingle."

"Yea, block away from the town square."

"That's right."

Her full head of brown hair looked like it did the night we met. She truly was gorgeous. Her jawline so defined and elegant, eyes with the same sparks and curving lights. There was something else endearing about her. Was it physical? No. It was something about her character. I think it was the innocent way in which she accepted me, like simply another tree in the forest, taken in solely for existing. This made me almost want to quit with the lies meant to protect myself and trust that she would still want to be with me. How good it would be to not have to put all that energy into facades. But every lesson I'd ever experienced taught me better. I wasn't good enough to play the game and win without faking it. Oh, why the hell does it have to be a game at all!

"You ok?"

She was smiling bashfully. I had been staring at her and—oh my god— hopefully didn't say anything out loud.

"Yes. Sorry. Your eyes they're just beautiful."

"Ohhhh how sweet of you." I didn't want to be sweet. Sweet never got me anywhere for very long.

Her hand patted my knee in a gesture meant to test the waters as she leaned forward and grabbed a slice of the pizza. I was worried that my eating might be gross to her somehow. It was always the type of thing I concerned myself with.

The rest of the night we talked more about each other's family. (I made up stories about my family, centering everything around the farmhouse I live in). We opened a bottle of red wine, a Merlot, from my cabinet and caught a classic movie. Believe it was Casablanca, don't recall for sure. Rebecca did rest her head on my shoulder during parts of it. Pretty much an uneventful, boring night. To be expected when it comes to my world.

Except, for the second time, D.R. did speak to me, during the movie on the couch.

She's pretty... you're ugly... doesn't that make her ugly too?... why would you want to be with her... she wants to be with the ugliness you are trying to leave behind...

He knew exactly how to reach me.

MORE CHILDHOOD

I F FOR NO other reason women are vulnerable because they are too emotional. Women can be a strong sex, but culture has fed them loads of crap, equating an abundance of emotions with virtue. Since it's true that emotions can tend to fluctuate so often and so drastically in people, how does it make sense to live one's life around them, basing so many decisions on how one responds emotionally to everything? Nurturing a drastically emotional personality in oneself is exhausting and leads to a chaotic life.

Do you think Rembrandt honed his style by painting only when he felt like it? Violinist Rachmaninoff; yea, he became masterful without discipline. He just played whenever the mood fit him. BULLSHIT.

Thinking back to my victims, every one of them I was able to exploit due to their emotional state. By showing me their emotions at every turn, I was able to gauge how to act, what to say. It was easy to lie and know when I *could* lie. What I mean is, the stories I told them came so easy because I had something to work with.

And when Rebecca showed me her hand: *So you said you were dealing with some things...* I didn't have to make anything up out of nowhere to try to pass it off as truth. I saw that she was searching for the truth, so what I was about to tell her would likely be accepted as such. And, even if she didn't fully trust me she would accept my explanation because she didn't want to believe I was lying. Some women aren't like this. Most are. This is a vulnerability; to accept another by default, assuming the best in them. The victims I chose assumed the best of me till their fateful end.

What does all this have to do with my childhood? Remember: I was an only child, no friends, an outcast with those around me—lonely, with a threateningly abusive atmosphere at home. If I was going to survive, I had to learn quickly. When my Father's hand was close to my face or when his voice raised I desperately needed to avoid the worst.

Neither my Father nor Mother finished high school, and they both came from simpler, poor families. Their thought process was basic. So I learned to read them and do it well. At times my own anger still got me in trouble, many times Dad performed his tirade anyway, but oftentimes I could quell the escalation. Even at age 8, it became my duty to "manage" Dad as best I could.

A defensive posture:

"Oh no Dad, I would never do that."

"Please don't be mad, I won't do it ever again."

Or sometimes, before he became too angry he could be reasoned with.

"Do you think that is the smart way to deal with it?"

"See Dad, next time just wait a bit longer first."

Of course, I had to be extremely careful confronting him like this.

Even though I remained an outcast of sorts and was uncomfortable communicating in everyday settings, as time went on, I learned to read all types of people. Thinking back, I see that was another way I managed as a teenager and young man, and it was reading people that helped me tap into the vulnerabilities in women most recently.

DATE TWO

BY "MOST RECENTLY" I mean two years ago to the day. That's when Rebecca became victim number one.

We rendezvoused for a second official date at Carmella's Italian Restaurant. I'd asked her to meet me at seven O'clock because I had to work late. (But I didn't have to work late.) Apparently overcoming small talk was still a hump we needed to get over, so more small talk we made. I soon made an inquiry:

"Why do you not go by Becky?" I had been curious since meeting her that night at Wine and Dines.

"I was going to explain that. Oh, if my Mom was here now she'd scald anyone who called me Becky." She laughed and put her hand on my arm. "She always told me, Rebecca is your name and you'd better never let me hear anyone calling you different." Her smile dissipated. "She's only been gone for three years. It's still hard sometimes."

"I'm sorry." I put my hand on her arm. "Your Dad?"

"He passed away like twelve years ago. We never got along...."

Blah blah blah. And passed away? Why can't you just say died? "He DIED." OR, "He's DEAD." It is a peeve of mine. Life is life, dying is dying. Be real.

Before we were even done with dinner she expressed her intent to come home with me.

"Maybe watch another movie," she said. I didn't buy it. All I had to do was stay in control and listen; *actively* listen so I could respond accordingly to get what I wanted. Blah blah she continued. Her bites of dinner were only a tiny pause, but in them I visualized kissing her and being naked in bed. A huge amount of pressure was multiplying within about my being able to perform. I grew angry at her for making me feel that pressure.

His presence—that teenage reject D.R. Melvin—shot straight up from my feet to my head. Made me quiver, then he spoke:

Relax, Dylan. Tonight you're gonna change your world.

"Change your world," he said. One only has a given number of years of life to do something remarkable. Then came D.R. at such a late stage of my life but still at an opportune time. I wondered, hoping he wouldn't know *all* my thoughts, if his presence was a hindrance to my aspirations. Could also be that his presence would open a door for me to finally grasp control of my existence. And from the start, he was a likable partner. No formalities required, he's familiar to me and I to him. Refreshing.

We got out of our cars—Rebecca looked up at my farmhouse like it was some grand colonial. For me, the sky's gray hue reflected off the two living room windows. There was young D.R., afraid to play, considering a streak of industriousness to impress Dad, knowing any attempt at that would fall short too. He stood in place. When he looked up from the gravel and saw me I came to. Rebecca was standing anxiously at the door.

"Need to use the bathroom?" I asked.

"No."

Soon as we entered the closed-in porch she turned, grabbed me, and pressed the biggest, wettest open-mouthed kiss into my face. Not my lips—my face. Her passion was more fitting than she could have ever known, and she broke just long enough to say, "I like you, Dylan."

All the while my mind was trying to register everything the voice was saying. Like a perverted demon, D.R. cheered me on. *She likes you!*

Keys in lock... door open... embracing... kissing... clothes coming off. Feelings of lust and passion overwhelmed us both. I grabbed her arm and pulled her, side-stepping us both to my bed as we kissed. Besides being so damn pretty, her lips tasted fresh and hot. I tempered my ferocious instincts until we got to my bed.

"Feel this," I commanded. I placed her hand on my penis. "Feel it?"

"Yeeesss. It's been so long."

Nothing was standing in my way. I ripped what was left of our clothes off and threw her on the bed.

D.R. was getting a thrill too. *If only she knew what you are capable of!*

No foreplay, no tenderness. Just in. "Ouch, easy Dylan!"

"Shut up!

There was seemingly no going back once I yelled those words. Her expression was one of fear and regret as if every realization hit her at once. The man she barely knew was holding her down and showing her no mercy.

I let go of my inhibitions and laughed. Freedom!

You have the power!

So beautiful, and I was in her! Possibly for one second, if that, a part of me wanted to stop. She was being invaded in an immoral way. I, however, was special. Whether the world recognized that fact or not, I was special. My time had come and I had a right to take it.

Don't let up... take what can be yours... don't be a reject... don't be a failure... don't be an outcast... get it... take it!

"I won't be a reject! I won't be a failure!"

Take it!

Her screams echoed around me, and soon I began to see the severity of her circumstances. Then her hoarse screams searched and begged for a savior. There was only me. The new me.

When I pushed up from her body she began to writhe away until I cupped both my hands around her neck. All my weight—down through my arms. All she could do was suck for air and scratch at my wrists. Didn't matter what she did. Not going to be a failure now.

Take it.. Take her!

Something gave way in her neck. I gasped then shivered.

This is real!

A couple of spastic twitches and she was done. It was as if I were being born again. I finished inside her and fell asleep.

OTHER THINGS

BEEN A FEW days since I've written. Troubling news. Seems the Sheriff of this shithole county found Rebecca's body, and they have a nickname for the killer: "The Eye Collector Killer". They were on the television a little while ago ranting about how horrific this is, how terrible whoever did this must be, and so on. And some forensic scientist figured out that her eyes had been removed *before* her body was put in her car and hidden. Had I known at the time there would be other victims after Rebecca, I would have buried her. I did, however, bury the others.

Before I forget, in the interest of continuity, you may have easily calculated that there was as much as two decades where you don't know what I was doing. Savvy of you. Following my divorce, from about age twenty-three to forty-seven, I behaved myself. I got a job at a local factory that made materials for mig, tig, and stick welding. Didn't set my sites high, I know. But long as I was willing to go to work every day on time and work up a sweat it was an easy job to get and hold. Besides, structure was something I needed, and many facets of the job could be done without being around others. After putting in a full year, the pay increased and was outstanding.

Eleven years was all I could stand of that atmosphere though. I'd even worked my way up to the most easy line coordinator position. All I had to do was make sure we had the men to work my shift, had the materials to produce, and prevent downtime. Tolerating the few people necessary eventually became too difficult for me.

In any case, I lived in the farmhouse with no mortgage, and because I closed up the many bedrooms the cost to heat it in the winter and cool it in the summer was cheap. I also sold fifty acres of the farmland to the nearest neighbor for a reasonable half a million. Combining that with my savings, money was not going to be an issue. I was a slob who pretty much did

nothing until I noticed myself sliding down. It was time to get out into the world again, and that's when I ended up at Wine and Dines that night I met Rebecca.

Moving on...

Of all the nooks and crannies and rooms in this old farmhouse, I value the basement the most. This is no finished basement. It was never intended to be lived in, as it only houses the water heater, electrical wiring and plumbing. And oh, the gas furnace is down here too. I love it here. Even though it's damp and musty its rock walls and concrete floor somehow make me feel secure. Let's see. Come down the stairs, pass the water heater on the left, then the furnace on the right. Clockwise around the furnace is my corner of the world. There's a solid metal workbench I got for a hundred dollars at a welder's auction years ago. (It was the only auction I ever attended; wanted to prove I could do it.) On an oak shelf high above my workbench, there are four glass jars, canning jars that is, filled with formaldehyde and an eyeball in each. Rebecca, Teri, Rachel, and Shay. I kept the first eye of Rebecca's I messed up, so technically there are five. I deserve to be reminded of the botch job I did. All my past failures I've managed to put away except that one. It's a reminder to never go back.

More about my farmhouse. In 1910, Grandpa built it with the help of a couple of neighbors that were members of the same co-op. Until grandpa died, it was a working farm. Corn came out of the fields mostly. Grandma was left enough from his will to stay there and be comfortable until the day she died. I was eight or nine I think... we had just returned from the funeral home. Mom and Dad had a heated argument about what to do with the farmhouse. Mom didn't see what use it was to keep it, and she was adamant to the point of aggressively expressing her opinion to Dad. It was very much out of character for her. She snapped off my clip-on tie and pointed toward my room. Their disagreement still made it to my ears.

"Just because we inherited the house doesn't mean we have to keep it," she told him. "How are we going to afford the upkeep and taxes?"

"How do you expect me to throw the house away? I grew up in it! Maybe we can move there."

"I did not say throw it away. I just do not want to move! Money is tight, and we need to think about our child's future."

"Oh! Now I'm a Father who don't care about his son."

"I didn't say that!"

The conflict continued long after I climbed into bed. Like all the other thousand times, I trembled and dripped with sweat over whether Mom would take her words too far, whether Dad would hit her. Hell, for all I knew he would kill her. So many nights I imagined that. Because of his uncontrollable rage, killing Mom didn't seem too far-fetched.

For me, it was one of the loneliest nights ever. A young boy was supposed to have a smiling Mother and Father who read a story to him and tucked the covers like a cocoon around his neck. If I didn't exist maybe Mom would have loved that farmhouse.

Not sure what changed Mom's mind, but a few months later we sold our house in town and moved.

Besides the basement, Grandpa built two cellars under the house. One a storm cellar, the other a root cellar. Both accessible from outside. Because my Father's generation had refrigerators, he never used the root cellar for vegetable storage. A curious kid, I was always looking for a new place to play, but Dad never allowed me down there.

By chance has anyone reading this thought that maybe Dad wasn't as bad as I make him out to be? I was a screwed-up kid, right? Read on.

Several years ago I scoured my memories of childhood life, and think Dad may have concocted a plan. Because many of his activities were mysterious, moving miles away from town seemed convenient for him.

"Don't go in there" "Don't touch that" "Don't ask questions". Maybe those were normal Fatherly things to say to a son, but more times than not me and Mom had no clue what he was doing.

Two days after I turned eighteen, Mom died. I came home from school one day and she was gone. Dad was heartless. "A stroke," he told me. Then he grabbed his cigarettes and walked to the barn. It was like Dad waited until I was eighteen so he didn't have to take care of me, then made Mom die somehow.

On the day of Mom's funeral, I waited in a new gray suit bought with my own money. It was important that Mom would think I'm a handsome young man and be proud of me. My hair was combed the way she would like, too. When Dad pulled into the driveway I met him outside.

"I'm ready, Dad." I watched him stroll by me and head to the barn as he lit a cigarette. He didn't even look in my direction.

"Already did it."

"What you mean you did it?"

"Cremated her." Still not looking at me. "It's done that's what I mean."

"Oh my god, how could you!"

"It's done."

"I didn't get to say goodbye!"

I bolted, stopped in his path and took a swing at his face. Out of nowhere, his fist struck my face first. Backward into the tall grass I fell.

"You got five minutes to pack your things and start walking. Take what you can carry, boy."

With only four weeks to go until my high school graduation Dad took away my chance to say goodbye to my Mom. Moments later I cried out loud while my trepid feet walked the pavement. I wanted to do the same thing to him that I did to the squirrel when I was ten. Oh, about that squirrel. I didn't finish that story.

THE REST ABOUT THE SQUIRREL AND MORE

W HEN I WOKE up the next morning (after the squirrel incident), it was Saturday, maybe ten o'clock or so. Mom was stirring, trying to be silent with her every move because Dad was still in bed. Mom and I wanted Dad to have his typical morning smoke from his pipe, eat something, then run some errands, (and do those things without an argument or fight.) That morning he did, without saying a word.

With him gone and in the company of my smiling Mom, I crunched through two bowls of Captain Crunch Cereal. My favorite. No stress. I had no idea what old tune Mom was humming, likely something from one of the vinyl records she kept upstairs.

Two choices were before me. I could watch cartoons and actually be able to hear them because Dad wouldn't make me limit the volume, or I could go outside and play. Since Dad had just left, I calculated I had time to do both. On a whim, I licked the milk off my spoon, slipped it in my pocket, then plopped my bowl into the sudsy dishwater in the sink. Being that there was other silverware in the sink, Mom wouldn't notice that I kept one spoon.

"Going out to play Mom."

"Stay right here around the house. Your Daddy comes back and can't find you, he'll tan your hide."

The spoon—from a cheap mail-order collection of silverware with our last initial engraved on the handle—cheap like everything else in my family... Dad's Malibu... our carpet... our television... it was all indicative of our cheap lives. Apathetic, ignorant, lacking communication skills and at times unfriendly are terms that come to mind when I think of how the neighbor-hood must've perceived us. We were outcasts. Poison. Cheap throwaways. Paper plates.

With the spoon in my right hand, I rounded the garage. Ants were marching in three orderly trails from beneath a foot-sized rock toward the animal carcass. It was still there.

Thankfully there were no maggots or beetles on the squirrel, at least none that I could see. I stood for what was surely ten minutes or more, studying the smashed flesh, startled that I had done such a deed.

My thumb rubbed back and forth on the spoon, working up the nerve. I had to know I could decide on my own without being prodded with Fathers anger and hate. From a place unknown, sudden courage warmed over me, and I laughed at myself because being nervous was silly. The courage continued to build up to a point of serenity. I held the spoon tight, unsure what I was going to do with it in the first place.

Right or wrong, I was about to act. No coercion, it was going to be *my* act!

I cupped my left hand around part of the rigid body and dug in with the spoon. The condition of the eye didn't matter, I only wanted it out. Through the gore of mangled flesh, I pressed the spoon deep, eventually twisting and grinding the metal against bone. Rocking the spoon back and forth seemed to be the thing to do. Half smashed, the eye fell out onto the grass. The spoon slipped from my fingers, bounced off my shoe, and landed in the alley.

I later despised myself for what I did to that animal. But, at the same time, I began to realize what being in control felt like. I could continue being a worthless, stray puzzle piece that would never fit into the big picture, or I could have this power whenever I wanted.

It was dusk when Dad came back home. In my imagination, I could hear Mom's terrified heart pounding in her chest. The goodness in her half expected an apology, as she had many times passed. Of course, she never got

one. Either Dad would unleash more fury, or he'd go to bed without a word. This time he went to bed.

And Mom went to her bed.

Using carbon paper my Mom gave me to trace images with, I went about discreetly tracing JC Penny catalog images—women from the lingerie section to be precise. Laying on my stomach on the floor, a bright lamp focused above me, I laid the carbon paper under the page I chose to trace, then a fresh sheet of paper under that.

I admired the beautiful, artful lines and curvaceous shapes of their figures. I learned a lot from keenly observing how a raised arm flowed down to an armpit, then further down to shape part of the breast—how, at the top of her legs, a naturally sensual "V" angled toward her mysterious place. I didn't know what secrets were hidden under her panties, but I vowed one day to know everything about it. I only needed to grow up fast, get away from my childhood prison, then I'd be free to explore. Part of me doubted I'd ever be able to overcome the lot life dealt to me, but if there was a way I'd find it!

Thinking back to that time, even then I wondered if my obsession was normal. When a woman crossed my path, I'd begin picking apart her body. How are her legs shaped? Are her arms shapely? Do her shoulders look nice? Is her butt round? Hell, does she even *have* an ass? For a boy only age ten, I was in a crazy frenzy all the time. I didn't know if other boys did things like I did or not.

Father usually kept the upstairs blocked off because he didn't want to pay to heat it in the winter, so I rarely ventured there. (My bedroom was on the ground floor, right next to his, with an open archway between.) In late summer, when temperatures were humid and reached the high 90s, it became unbearable in our house. But Dad figured out a solution. He could run the old industrial pedestal fan upstairs, open a window, and it would circulate a nice cooling draft throughout the entire house. So when Dad did turn on the fan, I was allowed to go upstairs for a short while. It was a calming buffer between me and him. There were things stored up there like old furniture, books, and boxes. And the doll.

At the top of the stairs, I'd go left to stand in front of the powerful fan and take in its mesmerizing hum. There is a thin steel wardrobe, somewhat rickety and painted with the same battleship gray as Dad painted the back porch. The kitchen table you'd see next is from the fifties, and nearly every inch of its surface is covered with salt & pepper shakers, plates, glasses and so on. On the next wall, gray shelving that held more garage sale types of dooDads. Most noteworthy was a card shuffler. I'd seen it work years before when Mom and Dad cared to socialize by playing euchre. Split the deck, lay one half in one side, other half on the other, then crank the handle. Rubber wheels pulled cards one by one into a pile in the center. In seconds each side was empty of cards. Shuffled. Sorry for the details; I find it intriguing.

Beyond that room was a sunroom. It is where I kept most of my old toys. But if you go back to the top of the stairs and cross to the other side, you see a much larger room.

Let's see. Against the wall stood a tall, brown plywood case (*not* battleship gray), just the right size for three long guns and two or three cardboard boxes of shells. There was a single bed, made up with layers of seemingly dozens of blankets collected from both sides of the family. Then, an old dresser with drawers crammed full of pictures, doilies, and other knick-knacks. A bookshelf was next, only three narrow shelves. Among the few dozen books, two books in particular I always pulled out. Like a view into another realm, they became gold to me.

1001 Magic Tricks You Can Do was one of the books. Even though I lacked much of the material to accomplish the tricks, I found some I could do. The bloody finger in a box, the disappearing salt shaker....a few others. For a short time, magic distracted my mind with something other than my sad world. The other book helped fill my mind too. I cannot remember the title, but it was about sex. Each time I opened this book, I was anxious and nervous about the world it would open up for me. An old book from the '40s or '50s, it was surprisingly straightforward. A bit over my head at first, I dissected the few hand-drawn diagrams and eventually things began to make sense. Since I was apparently at the beginning of an early puberty, the timing of this discovery could not have been better.

I walk past the tiny door that leads to the attic and there is a full-sized bed, again layered with blankets. Lying on the bed, with her head on a pillow, was the doll.

The nameless, kid-sized doll, maybe three and a half feet tall standing, wore tan shorts and a green shirt with brown horizontal stripes. Her bristly blonde hair was held into place by time, and I had to brush it away to see her face. I'd go through this ritual of feeling dirty and being tempted. I would read books or play with old toys until I worked up the courage to lower my pants and pretend. I had to be very careful moving her because Mom could notice such things.

A perverted child? Probably. But even that childish, immature mind of mine was foreseeing a future of struggling to break free. I was going to have to take advantage of every opportunity, fight to gain control and be different than circumstances allowed.

GETTING TERI

Very soon after I properly collected my souvenir from Rebecca's body and preserved it, I got the urge to have another date. This would become victim number two.

When I visualized all it would take to make it happen again, it looked like this: meet the woman, get acquainted, don't make a fool of myself, don't be boring AND be interesting, explain my damn life, hope that all works out so I can have a second date, all while maintaining her trust—then work everything out without getting caught. It was a huge undertaking, not to mention everything progressed too easily with Rebecca; could not let that make me complacent.

Therefore for my next victim, I chose a prostitute. A whore. I suppose using a whore is a stereotypical thing. But that list above? It all goes away. All I had to do is flash enough money to make her good with going to my house. Six hundred dollars would be my first offer—up to one thousand.

Before leaving I prepared by shining my enucleation spoon and filled a jar with formaldehyde for upcoming eye number two of my collection. I fed one end of a nylon rope under the mattress until it came out the other side. Then, leaving a loop, I went back under to where the rope started. Each end of the rope I tied to a dowel. Finally, I removed my license plate and screwed on an older one I bought at a garage sale.

I waited until the sun went down, and with one thousand bucks headed south on the highway. Number 1, there are no street whores in my town, and number 2, I wanted to be at least thirty minutes from home. A precautionary radius.

Once I picked a discreet parking spot about a block away, I sat and patiently watched. Three women meandered back and forth in front of a row of businesses. You had a small hardware store, a barbershop, a Chinese takeout, and bail bonds right on the corner. Ironic.

The women of the night weren't dressed like those you might see in the movies, but they were provocative enough. Two chain-smoked while the other sipped on a can of cola. It was the cola sipper that grabbed my interest.

Somewhere between platinum and blonde hair and denim shorts—love denim shorts—black high heels, button-down shirt with what looked like one button keeping it together. She had very shapely legs and a medium cup size, incase you're interested. Not a glamorous gal, but pretty. I waited to be one hundred percent sure she was there to do business and that I wasn't wrongly assuming her profession. When another car pulled to the curb to pick up the black-haired one, I knew.

After spending all this time with D.R. I take him for granted and have therefore forgotten to mention him. Yes, since that first Moment with Rebecca he has been with me, talking whenever he has something to say. Rarely do we disagree and when we do, he wins. We've had our troubles, but he has proven himself a dedicated partner.

As I coasted to a stop the girls squinted through my headlights.

"Hi." What else do you say to whores when you greet them? The one I liked saw that my focus was on her, so she stepped forward. Her eyes were green, a color I didn't have!

Perfect! D.R. Added his two cents.

"There you are," I spoke my words to D.R. but the girl heard me.

"Do I know you?"

"No, sorry."

"Well, my name's Teri."

It wasn't her true name but I didn't give her mine either.

"Derrick."

"Well Derrick, haven't seen you before. What you need, directions?"

I was nervous but needed to be bolder. If I wasn't, D.R. would tell me to be.

"You know what I'm looking for."

"Tell me."

I liked that she wasn't coming across as slutty.

"Two hours. What is it called, girlfriend experience?"

She stepped closer and hunched to see the rest of me. "Sure you don't just want a blow in your car? Fifty."

"No. I have six hundred for two hours."

Her face lit up. "You want GFE for two hours it's seven."

I nodded.

"Park, we'll go up." Teri tilted her head toward an apartment door.

"Oh uh, I was thinking my place."

"No way. I don't do outcall."

"Eight hundred." I felt cocky bartering for her sex.

Tara stood straight and judged my face. "Two hours...GFE... your place... how do I know you ain't crazy?"

"Ok, one grand. That's all I got."

"Show me."

I already had the thousand separated out, so I pulled it from the cubby hole next to my steering wheel and fanned out the bills. "All hundreds. Pick any of them. They're real. And I'm safe, but I understand why you'd ask."

"Why me?"

I told her the truth. "I love your green eyes. I need them."

Her friend expressed a concerned "Be careful" as Tara stepped into my car.

"See you in a couple hours," Teri told her.

You won't be seeing anything in a couple hours.

TERI AT HOME

EVEN THOUGH I offered her no reason to think I might be a crazy killer, the circumstances were still out of her norm, and the long drive to my remote farmhouse didn't ease her feelings. To keep her from having second thoughts I gave her the money first thing, and played alternative and pop from the big city radio station. No awkward silence or need for small talk.

Inside I offered her a drink. "Tasty well water here."

She shrugged. "Sure."

"I'll grab that for you and we can get started if you want. I mean, I'm not in a hurry but I don't want you to be afraid."

"It's quite a long way getting here. You normally this nice?"

"Trying to be sensitive to your situation."

While sipping from her glass she strolled to the master bedroom on her own to have a look. The decades-old maplewood bed was at the center, nicely made with a long old fashioned quilt draping to the floor. She looked at it for the longest minute.

"You don't like modern furniture?"

"Not much. They don't make things like they used to. See the dresser? Solid maple too." I hadn't considered her age, not for a second. She was twenty-nine or thirty; could have been my daughter. "You don't like it?"

"I do. I always had the sense that I was a spirit born in the wrong time. I should have been born in like 1950 or 60. Maybe before that."

D.R. didn't say a word, but he was with me, taking it all in. I wasn't going to let him down. For standing by me and showing me the way to freedom, this student was going to pass the test. At the bedside, I knocked my shoes off with the heel from my other foot and laid back.

"I've never done this before. Paid for sex, that is. I'll let you take charge."

She met me there and stroked my leg up and down several times.

"Slip out of your pants love."

By the time I took my pants and underwear off and turned to see her, she was standing in nothing but the shirt.

"Want to take this off of me?"

"I do."

Still one button. My fingers caressed her breasts upward as I pushed the shirt off her shoulders.

"Turned on, Derrick?"

My cock bounced up and tapped her stomach.

I nodded. "Pretty smile."

"And my green eyes you like."

She pressed me backward until my knees buckled against the bed.

"Go ahead and lay down sweetheart. You've been working that strenuous job all day, let me help you feel better."

Desire grew into impatience as I let her work.

Keep her trust a little bit longer.

What she was giving me with her mouth was amazing. Another first.

Anytime now... don't wait until she manages to make a fool of you...

I combed my fingers through her hair... working out the timing of my first move, anticipating her first gasps of fear when she realizes I'd crossed the line. The joy and power was all about to be mine again! But all at once, the power in me dissipated and left me feeling vulnerable and humble. Hurting Teri was the last thing I wanted to do. I wondered, did she have kids? Was she trying to make her life better too?

You going to be a failure now? I told you not to be a weak fool! You want to be a reject again go ahead, but don't expect me to hang around!

I cried out in fear. "No don't leave me D.R.!"

Teri's head rose with horror, her fateful look fully aware that something wasn't right.

I clenched a ball of hair tighter and yanked her up to me.

"Don't hurt me!"

Her face was blood red, and in her expression was hate, anger, regret. The more she saw of my eyes the more the terror grew in hers. Tears streamed down her cheeks. Beautiful.

Doesn't it feel good Dylan?

"So good."

"Please don't," she pleaded.

"Are you begging?"

"You can have back your money—please!"

One hand full of hair, the other cupped at her neck like a vise, I rolled her over.

"You sexy whore. Let me love you."

Before her body seized, she screamed for the last time. She was locked up like an old dry motor. Nothing was going to stand in my way. Me and D.R. wanted the same thing and I was going to give it to us.

You're not going to be a disappointment are you Dylan?

"No. I want you to be proud of me. Be proud of what I have done with our lives."

I invaded her despite a rigid body that fought to keep me out. She just gripped my quilt at her sides and stared into space while I had my way with her. Occasionally she let out a deep grunt.

Once I was finished exploring and enjoying her, I positioned her across the bed with her head tilted back over the edge of the mattress. With the loop of the rope around her neck, I tightened it by twisting the dowels at the other end.

It didn't make sense to me that she would be such a weak gal. To me it seemed as if her chosen profession would require her to grow a thick skin. I tested her, but no matter what I did she was like a mummy.

Spitting, slapping, poking, pinching—nothing caused her to flinch. Last attempt, I pinched her nipple and twisted. Nothing. No way anybody can fake that well. Yes, she was alive. Her breath was warm on my face and her pulse was fast and steady in her wrist. She *was* alive.

With nothing left to prepare and the enucleation spoon in hand (the spoon with the notch if you remember), I squatted bedside where her head tilted back.

Feel the power you hold over her...

So that you can admire my technique, here are the details:

In case she was at once inclined to jump, I held my knee against her forehead, and with the spoon firmly between my thumb and fingers, I saw the bullseye—that spot between the top of the eyeball and the socket— and aimed. I stabbed through the eyelid, angling away from the eyeball, rocking the spoon to catch the muscle in the notch to sever it.

Her breathing became heavier and she winced mildly. For the next couple minutes, I worked on each of the muscles until I felt the eyeball become free, then lifted it gently out into my other hand.

"Teri, I'm proud of you. Great job!"

She was my guest and lover for the entire night.

My third victim would prove to be a fighter.

TWO MONTHS AGO

TWO MONTHS AGO I stood in a clearing amid a clump of trees in the rear of my property. The cold downpour was fitting my mood. I'd been battling serious depression like never before. Sure, I held a power within me that was unreal. I was no longer *under* control I was *in* control and found a way to live without being a reject or a failure. Here I was, experiencing immense guilt because I used four women to accomplish this. How could I have performed such acts and not fully realized what I was doing at the time? What about my human psyche prevented me from stopping myself?

In tears I gazed upon a lush, rootless space at three unmarked graves: Teri, Rachel, and Shay (green, blue, gray). I was proud of my eye collection and what it represented for me, but tragedies were buried underground.

And perhaps it shouldn't have bothered me as much as it did, but there was something else. That same day, the obituaries mentioned the death of Robert Melvin, my Father. The least deserving, he lived many long years after Mom's death. Funny lives we have.

Like tic marks on a prison wall, the days of my life became visible and clear. I could count them each. It was me always trying to do more than just survive. I wanted to live, but wasn't equipped to live. I yearned to learn, but didn't know how to learn. Even to this very day, ripples from childhood trauma filter everything I experience. That is it. In between the ripples there is nothing.

So there I was, at their graves, shivering wet. There was a noticeable buildup inside me; a buildup to what, I was unsure. Maybe a better word is culmination—yes, a *culmination* of everything, every day, every event and every emotion contained in my disgusting life.

Are you weak now? You worthless stubborn child... want me to leave?

D.R. had pushed me too far.

"You know what? Go ahead and leave damn you!"

To get me to comply, D.R. became a bully. More and more he was treating me like an outcast, and I'd had enough of that. "Oh my god," the realization was a smack in the face. "I'm so stupid!" I thought D.R. had been there to support my freedom, to liberate me.

My legs ran fast as they could, back to the farmhouse, through the soggy cornstalks and the muddy field. Something was going to be my choice, MINE. At least for the next Moment, I was listening to nobody but ME. There was still a way I could confront Dad.

In the gray of dusk, my heart thumped hard in my chest. I dropped to my knees. "D.R. you say it! If you have anything to say, you say it now!"

D.R. said nothing.

I then cursed Dad. "Go ahead and die you coward!"

In the muddy muck, I crawled to the heavily rusted root cellar door, expecting Dad to yell at me at any Moment. "I told you I don't want you in there!"

"I don't care what you want anymore Dad."

As soon as the door slammed open, musty, damp dust rushed up. Some stuck to me, some blew past my face and some got caught in the rain and was pressed back down to the earth. Each step carefully in front of the other, down the solid wood steps.

The dirt floor was surprisingly free of crevices weeds and pebbles. To my right was large wood shelving built with heavy lumber and painted white. Nothing on them. I remembered how Grandma did it. Vegetables from the

garden would be rotated on a designated shelf. Vegetables that need the coolest temperatures would be stored on the lower shelves, others would be fine higher up.

A few cobwebs arched from the shelf to the floor joists above my head. Everything, so dark. I squinted my eyes for a Moment until my eyes adjusted, then took a few more steps.

"I'm not afraid of you anymore Dad. I disobeyed you and there is nothing you can do."

Assuming there was nothing noteworthy in the corners still too black to see, I turned to leave but stopped. D.R. had something to say. If I was no longer going to accept him, he was going to stab me with one last gesture of revenge.

Little D.R. stood before me, pointing back into the darkness.

You missed the best part of the tour.

"What?"

I know something you don't.

Of course, I didn't want to appease him, but I had to know.

"So, D.R., have you realized the error of your ways, are you helping me now? Or are you wanting to see me pay for disobeying?"

Stepping closer to the furthest corner, something glinted, barely. It was like that faint star in the black of space that disappears when you gaze directly at it. My toes tapped in front of me, testing my path as I slid forward one more half-step.

"No!"

Ha ha ha ha...

"No, no no!"

It was Mom's pearl necklace, still hanging around her neck. Poor Mom!

END

IT'S BEEN DAYS since I wrote that part about finding Mom in the root cellar. I still have bouts where I sob for hours. After considering payback on my Father's corpse, I concluded such an act would only add to how despicable I've been.

How Dad could have done such a horrible thing to Mom I'll never understand. Besides the pearl necklace, Dad had at least saw fit to have Mom in her favorite blue and white floral dress. The following day, with the ground still soft, I buried my Mother properly in the back of the house. I kissed her and told her she was pretty.

There is so much more I could have written. The amount of abuse I witnessed and absorbed will always be something I can't bring myself to completely open up about. In the end, I'm an adult child if you will, who only wanted to be more than a meaningless vapor in time. I chose to seek meaning at any violent cost, and wound up becoming the monster I had been working to avoid.

Right now the stories of Rachel and Shay will remain untold. Maybe, *maybe* I will write about them in a separate journal. Maybe hide it somewhere to be found some time. Then again, what's the point?

In the news there is an artist sketch of me floating around. It's pretty good. They're going to find me, and soon. And yes, I still hear D.R. speaking.

Be proud. You broke the mold, became more than you thought.

After all I've been through and all I've done to these women, I sit empty. Still a lifeless, formless human being with a voided soul.

Aren't you proud?

No I'm not proud! Why can't D.R. leave me alone instead of prodding me into anguish? He is no partner. He's a constant reminder of the monster I became. There is no way but one to shut him up, or perhaps I deserve to suffer the seconds away.

There is a commotion outside and a knock at the door.

Women employed as wipers during WW2 have lunch in the roundhouse in Clinton, Iowa.
(Between 1939-1945)

EDGAR ALLAN POE, born to actor parents on January 19, 1809, is best known for writing dark short stories and poetry. "The Raven", "The Tell-Tale Heart", and "The Fall of the House of Usher", are just a few of his recognized pieces of literature. Abraham Lincoln and Charles Darwin were also born in February of the same year. Other major events of 1809 include the inauguration of the fourth President of the United States, James Madison, and Mary Kies becomes the first woman to receive a patent for a technique of weaving straw with silk.

As much as Poe excelled in school and then college, he never completed his degree at the University of Virginia, due to debt. Poe joined the Army in 1827, and later the United States Military Academy in 1829, where yet again he had to leave due to lack of funds. Even though Poe was left to dismantle his endeavors in school and the military, he started to publish collections of poetry. He also went on to sell short stories like the one you are about to read, "The System of Doctor Tarr and Professor Fether"; a gothic comedy published in Graham's Magazine in November 1845.

I never attributed humor to this author. Yet, this enchantingly eccentric comedy, about a narrator's visit with a mixture of oddly curious characters within a mental asylum, made me snicker several times. In one particular scene, Poe's colorful description of the attendees at a dinner party was so amusing that I didn't want the written performance to end. If you read this story and yearn for more, then look for the movie, *Stonehearst Asylum*, starring Kate Beckinsale and Ben Kingsley. The movie takes elements of Poe's short story and twists it into a sinister tale regarding the relationship between mentally ill patients and their caretakers. The eeriness of the inner asylum lends itself to the similar feel of Poe's tale, but also includes some quirky humor along the way.

As a writer and avid reader, I strive to appreciate the greatness in a piece, but that doesn't mean I always become a fan of the author. However, after realizing Poe can so masterfully mix darkness with humor, I am now a new devotee. I hope you will look forward to reading more of his work as I now do.

Edgar Allan Poe's:

THE SYSTEM OF DOCTOR TARR AND PROFESSOR FETHER

During the autumn of 18—, while on a tour through the extreme southern provinces of France, my route led me within a few miles of a certain *Maison de Santé* or private mad-house, about which I had heard much, in Paris, from my medical friends. As I had never visited a place of the kind, I thought the opportunity too good to be lost; and so proposed to my traveling companion (a gentleman with whom I had made casual acquaintance a few days before), that we should turn aside, for an hour or so, and look through the establishment. To this he objected—pleading haste in the first place, and, in the second, a very usual horror at the sight of a lunatic. He begged me, however, not to let any mere courtesy towards himself interfere with the gratification of my curiosity, and said that he would ride on leisurely, so that I might overtake him during the day, or, at all events, during the next. As he bade me good-bye, I bethought me that there might be some difficulty in obtaining access to the premises, and mentioned my fears on this point. He replied that, in fact, unless I had personal knowledge of the superintendent, Monsieur Maillard, or some credential in the way of a letter, a difficulty might be found to exist, as the regulations of these private mad-houses were more rigid than the public hospital laws. For himself, he added, he had, some years since, made the acquaintance of Maillard, and would so far assist me as to ride up to the door and introduce me; although his feelings on the subject of lunacy would not permit of his entering the house.

I thanked him, and, turning from the main road, we entered a grass-grown by-path, which, in half an hour, nearly lost itself in a dense forest, clothing the base of a mountain. Through this dank and gloomy wood we rode some two miles, when the *Maison de Santé* came in view. It was a fantastic château, much dilapidated, and indeed scarcely tenantable through age and neglect. Its aspect inspired me with absolute dread, and, checking my horse, I half resolved to turn back. I soon, however, grew ashamed of my weakness, and proceeded.

As we rode up to the gate-way, I perceived it slightly open, and the visage of a man peering through. In an instant afterward, this man came forth, accosted my companion by name, shook him cordially by the hand, and begged him to alight. It was Monsieur Maillard himself. He was a portly, fine-looking gentleman of the old school, with a polished manner, and a certain air of gravity, dignity, and authority which was very impressive.

My friend, having presented me, mentioned my desire to inspect the establishment, and received Monsieur Maillard's assurance that he would show me all attention, now took leave, and I saw him no more.

When he had gone, the superintendent ushered me into a small and exceedingly neat parlor, containing, among other indications of refined taste, many books, drawings, pots of flowers, and musical instruments. A cheerful fire blazed upon the hearth. At a piano, singing an aria from Bellini, sat a young and very beautiful woman, who, at my entrance, paused in her song, and received me with graceful courtesy. Her voice was low, and her whole manner subdued. I thought, too, that I perceived the traces of sorrow in her countenance, which was excessively, although to my taste, not unpleasingly, pale. She was attired in deep mourning, and excited in my bosom a feeling of mingled respect, interest, and admiration.

I had heard, at Paris, that the institution of Monsieur Maillard was managed upon what is vulgarly termed the "system of soothing"—that all punishments were avoided—that even confinement was seldom resorted to—that the patients, while secretly watched, were left much apparent liberty, and that most of them were permitted to roam about the house and grounds in the ordinary apparel of persons in right mind.

Keeping these impressions in view, I was cautious in what I said before the young lady; for I could not be sure that she was sane; and, in fact, there was a certain restless brilliancy about her eyes which half led me to imagine she was not. I confined my remarks, therefore, to general topics, and to such as I thought would not be displeasing or exciting even to a lunatic. She replied in a perfectly rational manner to all that I said; and even her original observations were marked with the soundest good sense, but a long acquaintance with the metaphysics of mania, had taught me to put no faith in such evidence of sanity, and I continued to practise, throughout the interview, the caution with which I commenced it.

Presently a smart footman in livery brought in a tray with fruit, wine, and other refreshments, of which I partook, the lady soon afterward leaving the room. As she departed I turned my eyes in an inquiring manner toward my host.

"No," he said, "oh, no—a member of my family—my niece, and a most accomplished woman."

"I beg a thousand pardons for the suspicion," I replied, "but of course you will know how to excuse me. The excellent administration of your affairs here is well understood in Paris, and I thought it just possible, you know—"

"Yes, yes—say no more—or rather it is myself who should thank you for the commendable prudence you have displayed. We seldom find so much of forethought in young men; and, more than once, some unhappy contre-temps has occurred in consequence of thoughtlessness on the part of our visitors. While my former system was in operation, and my patients were permitted the privilege of roaming to and fro at will, they were often aroused to a dangerous frenzy by injudicious persons who called to inspect the house. Hence I was obliged to enforce a rigid system of exclusion; and none obtained access to the premises upon whose discretion I could not rely."

"While your former system was in operation!" I said, repeating his words—"do I understand you, then, to say that the 'soothing system' of which I have heard so much is no longer in force?"

"It is now," he replied, "several weeks since we have concluded to renounce it forever."

"Indeed! you astonish me!"

"We found it, sir," he said, with a sigh, "absolutely necessary to return to the old usages. The danger of the soothing system was, at all times, appalling; and its advantages have been much overrated. I believe, sir, that in this house it has been given a fair trial, if ever in any. We did every thing that rational humanity could suggest. I am sorry that you could not have paid us a visit at an earlier period, that you might have judged for yourself. But I presume you are conversant with the soothing practice—with its details."

"Not altogether. What I have heard has been at third or fourth hand."

"I may state the system, then, in general terms, as one in which the patients were *menagés*—humored. We contradicted no fancies which entered the brains of the mad. On the contrary, we not only indulged but encouraged them; and many of our most permanent cures have been thus effected. There is no argument which so touches the feeble reason of the madman as the *argumentum ad absurdum*. We have had men, for example, who fancied themselves chickens. The cure was, to insist upon the thing as a fact—to accuse the patient of stupidity in not sufficiently perceiving it to be a fact—and thus to refuse him any other diet for a week than that which properly appertains to a chicken. In this manner a little corn and gravel were made to perform wonders."

"But was this species of acquiescence all?"

"By no means. We put much faith in amusements of a simple kind, such as music, dancing, gymnastic exercises generally, cards, certain classes of books, and so forth. We affected to treat each individual as if for some ordinary physical disorder; and the word 'lunacy' was never employed. A great point was to set each lunatic to guard the actions of all the others. To repose confidence in the understanding or discretion of a madman, is to gain him body and soul. In this way we were enabled to dispense with an expensive body of keepers."

"And you had no punishments of any kind?"

"None."

"And you never confined your patients?"

"Very rarely. Now and then, the malady of some individual growing to a crisis, or taking a sudden turn of fury, we conveyed him to a secret cell, lest his disorder should infect the rest, and there kept him until we could dismiss him to his friends—for with the raging maniac we have nothing to do. He is usually removed to the public hospitals."

"And you have now changed all this—and you think for the better?"

"Decidedly. The system had its disadvantages, and even its dangers. It is now, happily, exploded throughout all the *Maisons de Santé* of France."

"I am very much surprised," I said, "at what you tell me; for I made sure that, at this moment, no other method of treatment for mania existed in any portion of the country."

"You are young yet, my friend," replied my host, "but the time will arrive when you will learn to judge for yourself of what is going on in the world, without trusting to the gossip of others. Believe nothing you hear, and only one-half that you see. Now about our *Maisons de Santé*, it is clear that some ignoramus has misled you. After dinner, however, when you have sufficiently recovered from the fatigue of your ride, I will be happy to take you over the house, and introduce to you a system which, in my opinion, and in that of every one who has witnessed its operation, is incomparably the most effectual as yet devised."

"Your own?" I inquired—"one of your own invention?"

"I am proud," he replied, "to acknowledge that it is—at least in some measure."

In this manner I conversed with Monsieur Maillard for an hour or two, during which he showed me the gardens and conservatories of the place.

"I cannot let you see my patients," he said, "just at present. To a sensitive mind there is always more or less of the shocking in such exhibitions; and I do not wish to spoil your appetite for dinner. We will dine. I can give you some veal a la Menehoult, with cauliflowers in *velouté* sauce—after that a glass of Clos de Vougeot—then your nerves will be sufficiently steadied."

At six, dinner was announced; and my host conducted me into a large *salle à manger*, where a very numerous company were assembled—twenty-five or thirty in all. They were, apparently, people of rank—certainly of high breeding—although their habiliments, I thought, were extravagantly rich, partaking somewhat too much of the ostentatious finery of the *vielle cour*. I noticed that at least two-thirds of these guests were ladies; and some of the latter were by no means accoutred in what a Parisian would consider good taste at the present day. Many females, for example, whose age could not have been less than seventy were bedecked with a profusion of jewelry, such as rings, bracelets, and earrings, and wore their bosoms and arms shamefully bare. I observed, too, that very few of the dresses were well made—or, at least, that very few of them fitted the wearers. In looking about, I discovered the interesting girl to whom Monsieur Maillard had presented me in the little parlor; but my surprise was great to see her wearing a hoop and farthingale, with high-heeled shoes, and a dirty cap of Brussels lace, so much too large for her that it gave her face a ridiculously diminutive expression. When I had first seen her, she was attired, most becomingly, in deep mourning. There was an air of oddity, in short, about the dress of the whole party, which, at first, caused me to recur to my original idea of the "soothing system," and to fancy that Monsieur Maillard had been willing to deceive me until after dinner, that

I might experience no uncomfortable feelings during the repast, at finding myself dining with lunatics; but I remembered having been informed, in Paris, that the southern provincialists were a peculiarly eccentric people, with a vast number of antiquated notions; and then, too, upon conversing with several members of the company, my apprehensions were immediately and fully dispelled.

The dining-room itself, although perhaps sufficiently comfortable and of good dimensions, had nothing too much of elegance about it. For example, the floor was uncarpeted; in France, however, a carpet is frequently dispensed with. The windows, too, were without curtains; the shutters, being shut, were securely fastened with iron bars, applied diagonally, after the fashion of our ordinary shop-shutters. The apartment, I observed, formed, in itself, a wing of the château, and thus the windows were on three sides of the parallelogram, the door being at the other. There were no less than ten windows in all.

The table was superbly set out. It was loaded with plate, and more than loaded with delicacies. The profusion was absolutely barbaric. There were meats enough to have feasted the Anakim. Never, in all my life, had I witnessed so lavish, so wasteful an expenditure of the good things of life. There seemed very little taste, however, in the arrangements; and my eyes, accustomed to quiet lights, were sadly offended by the prodigious glare of a multitude of wax candles, which, in silver candelabra, were deposited upon the table, and all about the room, wherever it was possible to find a place. There were several active servants in attendance; and, upon a large table, at the farther end of the apartment, were seated seven or eight people with fiddles, fifes, trombones, and a drum. These fellows annoyed me very much, at intervals, during the repast, by an infinite variety of noises, which were intended for music, and which appeared to afford much entertainment to all present, with the exception of myself.

Upon the whole, I could not help thinking that there was much of the bizarre about every thing I saw—but then the world is made up of all kinds of persons, with all modes of thought, and all sorts of conventional customs. I had travelled, too, so much, as to be quite an adept at the nil admirari; so I took my seat very coolly at the right hand of my host, and, having an excellent appetite, did justice to the good cheer set before me.

The conversation, in the meantime, was spirited and general. The ladies, as usual, talked a great deal. I soon found that nearly all the company were well educated; and my host was a world of good-humored anecdote in himself. He seemed quite willing to speak of his position as superintendent of a *Maison de Santé*; and, indeed, the topic of lunacy was, much to my surprise, a favorite one with all present. A great many amusing stories were told, having reference to the *whims* of the patients.

"We had a fellow here once," said a fat little gentleman, who sat at my right,—"a fellow that fancied himself a tea-pot; and by the way, is it not especially singular how often this particular crotchet has entered the brain of the lunatic? There is scarcely an insane asylum in France which cannot supply a human tea-pot. Our gentleman was a Britannia-ware tea-pot, and was careful to polish himself every morning with buckskin and whiting."

"And then," said a tall man just opposite, "we had here, not long ago, a person who had taken it into his head that he was a donkey—which allegorically speaking, you will say, was quite true. He was a troublesome patient; and we had much ado to keep him within bounds. For a long time he would eat nothing but thistles; but of this idea we soon cured him by insisting upon his eating nothing else. Then he was perpetually kicking out his heels—so—so—"

"Mr. De Kock! I will thank you to behave yourself!" here interrupted an old lady, who sat next to the speaker. "Please keep your feet to yourself! You have spoiled my brocade! Is it necessary, pray, to illustrate a remark in so practical a style? Our friend here can surely comprehend you without all this. Upon my word, you are nearly as great a donkey as the poor unfortunate imagined himself. Your acting is very natural, as I live."

"Mille pardons! Ma'm'selle!" replied Monsieur De Kock, thus addressed—"a thousand pardons! I had no intention of offending. Ma'm'selle Laplace—Monsieur De Kock will do himself the honor of taking wine with you."

Here Monsieur De Kock bowed low, kissed his hand with much ceremony, and took wine with Ma'm'selle Laplace.

"Allow me, mon ami," now said Monsieur Maillard, addressing myself, "allow me to send you a morsel of this veal *à la St. Menehoult*—you will find it particularly fine."

At this instant three sturdy waiters had just succeeded in depositing safely upon the table an enormous dish, or trencher, containing what I supposed to be the "*monstrum, horrendum, informe, ingens, cui lumen ademptum.*" A closer scrutiny assured me, however, that it was only a small calf roasted whole, and set upon its knees, with an apple in its mouth, as is the English fashion of dressing a hare.

"Thank you, no," I replied; "to say the truth, I am not particularly partial to veal *à la St.*—what is it?—for I do not find that it altogether agrees with me. I will change my plate, however, and try some of the rabbit."

There were several side-dishes on the table, containing what appeared to be the ordinary French rabbit—a very delicious morceau, which I can recommend.

"Pierre," cried the host, "change this gentleman's plate, and give him a side-piece of this rabbit au-chat."

"This what?" said I.

"This rabbit *au-chat.*"

"Why, thank you—upon second thoughts, no. I will just help myself to some of the ham."

There is no knowing what one eats, thought I to myself, at the tables of these people of the province. I will have none of their rabbit *au-chat*—and, for the matter of that, none of their *cat-au-rabbit* either.

"And then," said a cadaverous looking personage, near the foot of the table, taking up the thread of the conversation where it had been broken off,—"and then, among other oddities, we had a patient, once upon a time, who very pertinaciously maintained himself to be a Cordova cheese, and went about, with a knife in his hand, soliciting his friends to try a small slice from the middle of his leg."

"He was a great fool, beyond doubt," interposed some one, "but not to be compared with a certain individual whom we all know, with the exception of this strange gentleman. I mean the man who took himself for a bottle of champagne, and always went off with a pop and a fizz, in this fashion."

Here the speaker, very rudely, as I thought, put his right thumb in his left cheek, withdrew it with a sound resembling the popping of a cork, and then, by a dexterous movement of the tongue upon the teeth, created a sharp hissing and fizzing, which lasted for several minutes, in imitation of the frothing of champagne. This behavior, I saw plainly, was not very pleasing to Monsieur Maillard; but that gentleman said nothing, and the conversation was resumed by a very lean little man in a big wig.

"And then there was an ignoramus," said he, "who mistook himself for a frog, which, by the way, he resembled in no little degree. I wish you could have seen him, sir,"—here the speaker addressed myself—"it would have done your heart good to see the natural airs that he put on. Sir, if that man was not a frog, I can only observe that it is a pity he was not. His croak thus—o-o-o-o-gh—o-o-o-o-gh! was the finest note in the world—B flat; and when he put his elbows upon the table thus—after taking a glass or two of wine—and distended his mouth, thus, and rolled up his eyes, thus, and winked them with excessive rapidity, thus, why then, sir, I take it upon myself to say, positively, that you would have been lost in admiration of the genius of the man."

"I have no doubt of it," I said.

"And then," said somebody else, "then there was Petit Gaillard, who thought himself a pinch of snuff, and was truly distressed because he could not take himself between his own finger and thumb."

"And then there was Jules Desoulières, who was a very singular genius, indeed, and went mad with the idea that he was a pumpkin. He persecuted the cook to make him up into pies—a thing which the cook indignantly refused to do. For my part, I am by no means sure that a pumpkin pie *à la Desoulières* would not have been very capital eating indeed!"

"You astonish me!" said I; and I looked inquisitively at Monsieur Maillard.

"Ha! ha! ha!" said that gentleman—"he! he! he!—hi! hi! hi!—ho! ho! ho!—hu! hu! hu!—very good indeed! You must not be astonished, *mon ami;* our friend here is a wit—a *drôle*—you must not understand him to the letter."

"And then," said some other one of the party,—"then there was Bouffon Le Grand—another extraordinary personage in his way. He grew deranged through love, and fancied himself possessed of two heads. One of these he maintained to be the head of Cicero; the other he imagined a composite one, being Demosthenes' from the top of the forehead to the mouth, and Lord Brougham's from the mouth to the chin. It is not impossible that he was wrong; but he would have convinced you of his being in the right; for he was a man of great eloquence. He had an absolute passion for oratory, and could not refrain from display. For example, he used to leap upon the dinner-table thus, and—and—"

Here a friend, at the side of the speaker, put a hand upon his shoulder and whispered a few words in his ear; upon which he ceased talking with great suddenness, and sank back within his chair.

"And then," said the friend who had whispered, "there was Boullard, the tee-totum. I call him the tee-totum because, in fact, he was seized with the droll, but not altogether irrational, crotchet, that he had been converted into a tee-totum. You would have roared with laughter to see him spin. He would turn round upon one heel by the hour, in this manner—so—"

Here the friend whom he had just interrupted by a whisper, performed an exactly similar office for himself.

"But then," cried the old lady, at the top of her voice, "your Monsieur Boullard was a madman, and a very silly madman at best; for who, allow me to ask you, ever heard of a human tee-totum? The thing is absurd. Madame Joyeuse was a more sensible person, as you know. She had a crotchet, but it was instinct with common sense, and gave pleasure to all who had the honor of her acquaintance. She found, upon mature deliberation, that, by some accident, she had been turned into a chicken-cock; but, as such, she behaved with propriety. She flapped her wings with prodigious effect—so—so—so—and, as for her crow, it was delicious! Cock-a-doodle-doo!—cock-a-doodle-doo!—cock-a-doodle-de-doo dooo-do-o-o-o-o-o-o!"

"Madame Joyeuse, I will thank you to behave yourself!" here interrupted our host, very angrily. "You can either conduct yourself as a lady should do, or you can quit the table forthwith—take your choice."

The lady (whom I was much astonished to hear addressed as Madame Joyeuse, after the description of Madame Joyeuse she had just given) blushed up to the eyebrows, and seemed exceedingly abashed at the reproof. She hung down her head, and said not a syllable in reply. But another and younger lady resumed the theme. It was my beautiful girl of the little parlor.

"Oh, Madame Joyeuse was a fool!" she exclaimed, "but there was really much sound sense, after all, in the opinion of Eugénie Salsafette. She was a very beautiful and painfully modest young lady, who thought the ordinary mode of habiliment indecent, and wished to dress herself, always, by getting outside instead of inside of her clothes. It is a thing very easily done, after all. You have only to do so—and then so—so—so—and then so—so—so—and then so—so—and then—"

"Mon dieu! Ma'm'selle Salsafette!" here cried a dozen voices at once. "What are you about?—forbear!—that is sufficient!—we see, very plainly, how it is done!—hold! hold!" and several persons were already leaping from their seats to withhold Ma'm'selle Salsafette from putting herself upon a par with the Medicean Venus, when the point was very effectually and suddenly accomplished by a series of loud screams, or yells, from some portion of the main body of the *château.*

My nerves were very much affected, indeed, by these yells; but the rest of the company I really pitied. I never saw any set of reasonable people so thoroughly frightened in my life. They all grew as pale as so many corpses, and, shrinking within their seats, sat quivering and gibbering with terror, and listening for a repetition of the sound. It came again—louder and seemingly nearer—and then a third time very loud, and then a fourth time with a vigor evidently diminished. At this apparent dying away of the noise, the spirits of the company were immediately regained, and all was life and anecdote as before. I now ventured to inquire the cause of the disturbance.

"A mere *bagatelle,*" said Monsieur Maillard. "We are used to these things, and care really very little about them. The lunatics, every now and then, get up a howl in concert; one starting another, as is sometimes the case with a bevy of dogs at night. It occasionally happens, however, that the *concerto* yells are succeeded by a simultaneous effort at breaking loose; when, of course, some little danger is to be apprehended."

"And how many have you in charge?"

"At present we have not more than ten, altogether."

"Principally females, I presume?"

"Oh, no—every one of them men, and stout fellows, too, I can tell you."

"Indeed! I have always understood that the majority of lunatics were of the gentler sex."

"It is generally so, but not always. Some time ago, there were about twenty-seven patients here; and, of that number, no less than eighteen were women; but, lately, matters have changed very much, as you see."

"Yes—have changed very much, as you see," here interrupted the gentleman who had broken the shins of Ma'm'selle Laplace.

"Yes—have changed very much, as you see!" chimed in the whole company at once.

"Hold your tongues, every one of you!" said my host, in a great rage. Whereupon the whole company maintained a dead silence for nearly a minute. As for one lady, she obeyed Monsieur Maillard to the letter, and thrusting out her tongue, which was an excessively long one, held it very resignedly, with both hands, until the end of the entertainment.

"And this gentlewoman," said I, to Monsieur Maillard, bending over and addressing him in a whisper—"this good lady who has just spoken, and who gives us the cock-a-doodle-de-doo—she, I presume, is harmless—quite harmless, eh?"

"Harmless!" ejaculated he, in unfeigned surprise, "why—why, what can you mean?"

"Only slightly touched?" said I, touching my head. "I take it for granted that she is not particularly not dangerously affected, eh?"

"*Mon dieu!* what is it you imagine? This lady, my particular old friend Madame Joyeuse, is as absolutely sane as myself. She has her little eccentricities, to be sure—but then, you know, all old women—all *very* old women—are more or less eccentric!"

"To be sure," said I,—"to be sure—and then the rest of these ladies and gentlemen—"

"Are my friends and keepers," interupted Monsieur Maillard, drawing himself up with *hauteur*,—"my very good friends and assistants."

"What! all of them?" I asked,—"the women and all?"

"Assuredly," he said,—"we could not do at all without the women; they are the best lunatic nurses in the world; they have a way of their own, you know; their bright eyes have a marvellous effect—something like the fascination of the snake, you know."

"To be sure," said I,—"to be sure! They behave a little odd, eh?—they are a little queer, eh?—don't you think so?"

"Odd!—queer!—why, do you really think so? We are not very prudish, to be sure, here in the South—do pretty much as we please—enjoy life, and all that sort of thing, you know—"

"To be sure," said I,—"to be sure."

"And then, perhaps, this Clos de Vougeot is a little heady, you know—a little strong—you understand, eh?"

"To be sure," said I,—"to be sure. By the bye, Monsieur, did I understand you to say that the system you have adopted, in place of the celebrated soothing system, was one of very rigorous severity?"

"By no means. Our confinement is necessarily close; but the treatment—the medical treatment, I mean—is rather agreeable to the patients than otherwise."

"And the new system is one of your own invention?"

"Not altogether. Some portions of it are referable to Professor Tarr, of whom you have, necessarily, heard; and, again, there are modifications in my plan which I am happy to acknowledge as belonging of right to the celebrated Fether, with whom, if I mistake not, you have the honor of an intimate acquaintance."

"I am quite ashamed to confess," I replied, "that I have never even heard the names of either gentleman before."

"Good heavens!" ejaculated my host, drawing back his chair abruptly, and uplifting his hands. "I surely do not hear you aright! You did not intend to say, eh? that you had never heard either of the learned Doctor Tarr, or of the celebrated Professor Fether?"

"I am forced to acknowledge my ignorance," I replied; "but the truth should be held inviolate above all things. Nevertheless, I feel humbled to the dust, not to be acquainted with the works of these, no doubt, extraordinary men. I will seek out their writings forthwith, and peruse them with deliberate care. Monsieur Maillard, you have really—I must confess it—you have really—made me ashamed of myself!"

And this was the fact.

"Say no more, my good young friend," he said kindly, pressing my hand,—"join me now in a glass of Sauterne."

We drank. The company followed our example without stint. They chatted—they jested—they laughed—they perpetrated a thousand absurdities—the fiddles shrieked—the drum row-de-dowed—the trombones bellowed like so many brazen bulls of Phalaris—and the whole scene, growing gradually worse and worse, as the wines gained the ascendancy, became at length a sort of pandemonium in petto. In the meantime, Monsieur Maillard and myself, with some bottles of Sauterne and Vougeot between us, continued our conversation at the top of the voice. A word spoken in an ordinary key stood no more chance of being heard than the voice of a fish from the bottom of Niagara Falls.

"And, sir," said I, screaming in his ear, "you mentioned something before dinner about the danger incurred in the old system of soothing. How is that?"

"Yes," he replied, "there was, occasionally, very great danger indeed. There is no accounting for the caprices of madmen; and, in my opinion as well as in that of Dr. Tarr and Professor Fether, it is never safe to permit them to run at large unattended. A lunatic may be 'soothed,' as it is called, for a time, but, in the end, he is very apt to become obstreperous. His cunning, too, is proverbial and great. If he has a project in view, he conceals his design with a marvellous wisdom; and the dexterity with which he counterfeits sanity, presents, to the metaphysician, one of the most singular problems in the study of mind. When a madman appears thoroughly sane, indeed, it is high time to put him in a straitjacket."

"But the danger, my dear sir, of which you were speaking, in your own experience—during your control of this house—have you had practical reason to think liberty hazardous in the case of a lunatic?"

"Here?—in my own experience?—why, I may say, yes. For example:—no very long while ago, a singular circumstance occurred in this very house. The 'soothing system,' you know, was then in operation, and the patients were at large. They behaved remarkably well—especially so—any one of sense might have known that some devilish scheme was brewing from that particular fact, that the fellows behaved so remarkably well. And, sure enough, one fine morning the keepers found themselves pinioned hand and foot, and thrown into the cells, where they were attended, as if they were the lunatics, by the lunatics themselves, who had usurped the offices of the keepers."

"You don't tell me so! I never heard of any thing so absurd in my life!"

"Fact—it all came to pass by means of a stupid fellow—a lunatic—who, by some means, had taken it into his head that he had invented a better system of government than any ever heard of before—of lunatic government, I mean. He wished to give his invention a trial, I suppose, and so he persuaded the rest of the patients to join him in a conspiracy for the overthrow of the reigning powers."

"And he really succeeded?"

"No doubt of it. The keepers and kept were soon made to exchange places. Not that exactly either—for the madmen had been free, but the keepers were shut up in cells forthwith, and treated, I am sorry to say, in a very cavalier manner."

"But I presume a counter-revolution was soon effected. This condition of things could not have long existed. The country people in the neighborhood—visitors coming to see the establishment—would have given the alarm."

"There you are out. The head rebel was too cunning for that. He admitted no visitors at all—with the exception, one day, of a very stupid-looking young gentleman of whom he had no reason to be afraid. He let him in to see the place—just by way of variety,—to have a little fun with him. As soon as he had gammoned him sufficiently, he let him out, and sent him about his business."

"And how long, then, did the madmen reign?"

"Oh, a very long time, indeed—a month certainly—how much longer I can't precisely say. In the meantime, the lunatics had a jolly season of it—that you may swear. They doffed their own shabby clothes, and made free with the family wardrobe and jewels. The cellars of the château were well stocked with wine; and these madmen are just the devils that know how to drink it. They lived well, I can tell you."

"And the treatment—what was the particular species of treatment which the leader of the rebels put into operation?"

"Why, as for that, a madman is not necessarily a fool, as I have already observed; and it is my honest opinion that his treatment was a much better treatment than that which it superseded. It was a very capital system indeed—simple—neat—no trouble at all—in fact it was delicious—it was—"

Here my host's observations were cut short by another series of yells, of the same character as those which had previously disconcerted us. This time, however, they seemed to proceed from persons rapidly approaching.

"Gracious heavens!" I ejaculated—"the lunatics have most undoubtedly broken loose."

"I very much fear it is so," replied Monsieur Maillard, now becoming excessively pale. He had scarcely finished the sentence, before loud shouts and imprecations were heard beneath the windows; and, immediately afterward, it became evident that some persons outside were endeavoring to gain entrance into the room. The door was beaten with what appeared to be a sledge-hammer, and the shutters were wrenched and shaken with prodigious violence.

A scene of the most terrible confusion ensued. Monsieur Maillard, to my excessive astonishment threw himself under the side-board. I had expected more resolution at his hands. The members of the orchestra, who, for the last fifteen minutes, had been seemingly too much intoxicated to do duty, now sprang all at once to their feet and to their instruments, and, scrambling upon their table, broke out, with one accord, into, "Yankee Doodle," which they performed, if not exactly in tune, at least with an energy superhuman, during the whole of the uproar.

Meantime, upon the main dining-table, among the bottles and glasses, leaped the gentleman who, with such difficulty, had been restrained from leaping there before. As soon as he fairly settled himself, he commenced an oration, which, no doubt, was a very capital one, if it could only have been heard. At the same moment, the man with the teetotum predilection, set himself to spinning around the apartment, with immense energy, and with arms outstretched at right angles with his body; so that he had all the air of a tee-totum in fact, and knocked everybody down that happened to get in his way. And now, too, hearing an incredible popping and fizzing of champagne, I discovered at length, that it proceeded from the person who performed the bottle of that delicate drink during dinner. And then, again, the frog-man croaked away as if the salvation of his soul depended upon every note that he uttered. And, in the midst of all this, the continuous braying of a donkey arose over all. As for my old friend, Madame Joyeuse, I really could have wept for the poor lady, she appeared so terribly perplexed. All she did, however, was to stand up in a corner, by the fireplace, and sing out incessantly at the top of her voice, "Cock-a-doodle-de-dooooooh!"

And now came the climax—the catastrophe of the drama. As no resistance, beyond whooping and yelling and cock-a-doodling, was offered to the encroachments of the party without, the ten windows were very speedily, and almost simultaneously, broken in. But I shall never forget the emotions of wonder and horror with which I gazed, when, leaping through these windows, and down among us *pêle-mêle*, fighting, stamping, scratching, and howling, there rushed a perfect army of what I took to be chimpanzees, ourang-outangs, or big black baboons of the Cape of Good Hope.

I received a terrible beating—after which I rolled under a sofa and lay still. After lying there some fifteen minutes, during which time I listened with all my ears to what was going on in the room, I came to same satisfactory *dénouement* of this tragedy. Monsieur Maillard, it appeared, in giving me the account of the lunatic who had excited his fellows to rebellion, had been merely relating his own exploits. This gentleman had, indeed, some two or three years before, been the superintendent of the establishment, but grew crazy himself, and so became a patient. This fact was unknown to the travelling companion who introduced me. The keepers, ten in number, having been suddenly overpowered, were first well tarred, then carefully feathered, and then shut up in underground cells. They had been so imprisoned for more than a month, during which period Monsieur Maillard had generously allowed them not only the tar and feathers (which constituted his "system"), but some bread and abundance of water. The latter was pumped on them daily. At length, one escaping through a sewer, gave freedom to all the rest.

The "soothing system," with important modifications, has been resumed at the *château;* yet I cannot help agreeing with Monsieur Maillard, that his own "treatment" was a very capital one of its kind. As he justly observed, it was "simple—neat—and gave no trouble at all—not the least."

I have only to add that, although I have searched every library in Europe for the works of Doctor *Tarr* and Professor *Fether*, I have, up to the present day, utterly failed in my endeavors at procuring an edition.

Orchard Corset

OrchardCorset.com
Ph. 1-866-456-7411

Corsets to suit your purpose:
waist training, weddings, costumes,
back pain relief, or just for fun.

04/23/19
Customer service and sizing experts
Customer service and sizing experts are very helpful and responsive. Feeling great about my order!
koma876omen

04/25/19
Very comfortable
Fits like a glove and is super comfortable. Highly recommend for daily use.
Dayna L.

04/24/19
Gorgeous!
I knew I had to get this one when I saw the teaser picture for it. It's even more gorgeous in person. Fits well even though I have...
Read More
Amy H.

-Sizing Experts Available 7 Days a Week
-Only Steel-Boned Corsets, Never Plastic
-Interest Free Pay Over Time Option!
-Rewards program
-Men's Corsets too

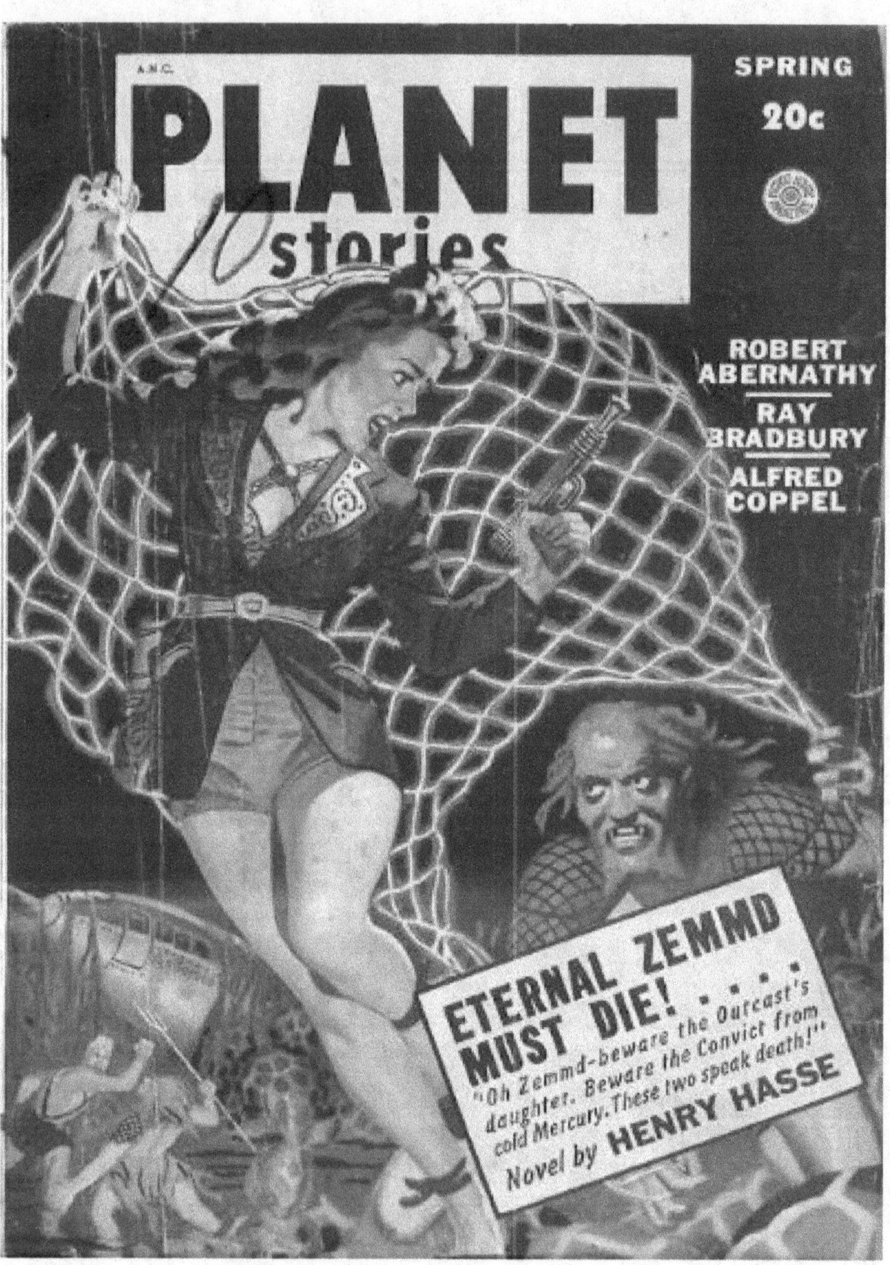

*Despite no mention of it on the cover, the following story
was included in this issue from Spring, 1949.*

<INTRODUCTION>
BY ROBERT KIMBRELL

STANLEY MULLEN WAS born in 1911, in Colorado Springs. Among current in events in that year: the first Indianapolis 500 was run, Machu Picchu is rediscovered by a man named Hiram Bingham, and Orville Wright set a world record by remaining in the air with his glider for over 9 minutes.

Drawing and painting were among Stanley Mullen's studies at the Fine Arts Center of Colorado Springs. If you happen by the Denver Art Museum, you can see a permanently displayed collection of his brush strokes.

Regarding Mullen's writing, the first thing I noticed is that it assumes you are familiar with the setting and the objects in the fantasy world. Writing good science fiction is an undertaking already, but when an author must find a way to artistically define what an unfamiliar item is, or precisely what it looks like, while at the same time not interrupting the cadence, it's doubly difficult. Don't fear, however, because due to the author's style, the story flows very well. When an unfamiliar item or word is introduced, you aren't left wondering what it is, because the author offers masterful context—without making it obvious. Second, I was taught that when writing scenes in which a physical fight takes place, not every move—uppercut—jab—needs to be stated. This is oftentimes true, because the reader naturally tends to fill in parts of heavy action scenes, and so being overly detailed can actually become monotonous and dull. In the case here, fight scenes are rather detailed, yet, it seems to add to the realism of the scene and not be a negative. These are my opinions, and it makes for a refreshing SciFi read.

As far as his writings go, if you include his other pen names, Mullen wrote over 200 stories as well as articles. Stanley Mullen died in 1974. His wonderful imagination can create worlds no more.

Many stories by Mullen are still very much available, so I will be enjoying more from this creator. I found Lady Into Hell-Cat to be a delightful science fiction adventure. By reading on, you will experience a world that is still out there, somewhere. And nothing like it can ever be created again.

LADY INTO HELL-CAT

BY STANLEY MULLEN

Tracking her across black space-lanes and slapping
magnetic bracelets on her was duck soup
for S.P. Agent Heydrick.

Only then did he learn what a planet-load
of trouble he'd bought.

THE INSPECTOR OF security police dropped his shoes on the floor and put his feet on the desk where he could watch his toes wriggle.

"Sure we're sloppy here," he said belligerently. "You pretty boys of the Space Patrol don't know what it's like in a slime-hole frontier town like 9 Ganymede."

Lee Heydrick smiled grimly. "I guess you didn't catch my name. I earned these service bars of mine. I was one of four survivors of the first Trans-Plutonian Expedition."

The inspector suddenly became respectful. "Oh, you're that Heydrick?" He referred to the credentials on his desk. "What's a pirate-chaser like you doing on an assignment like this? Seems like picking up fugitive murderers for the disintegrators is a job for the security police."

Heydrick grunted. "So it is. I don't like the job any better than you do. But this is no ordinary murderer. She's a red Martian. Killed Feyjak, third man in the Red Council. Worked in his laboratory. They suspect a Wilding plot."

"Feyjak, eh? They ought to give her a medal. I feel sorry for the girl—good-looker, too. Still sounds like a police job."

Heydrick growled. "Yes, it does. Just some more rotten politics. There's not supposed to be any politics in the Space Patrol. Hooey! The Red Scientists are in power, and my foster father, Tyko, is head man of the Blue. So I get assignments like this. Just so they can get a whack at Tyko. They hope I'll fail—that's all they want."

The inspector warmed noticeably. "So Tyko's your foster? I'm a blue myself ... out of working hours. That's why I'm stuck in a last frontier hellhole like this. Anything I can do to help?"

Heydrick loosened up and sat down. "I don't know. It's a mean job any way you look at it. The girl says she didn't kill him. They can't use scopolamine. She's a desert dweller of the old blood, and it doesn't work on 'em. Why would she kill Feyjak? He wasn't a bad sort. A bit dim, but that's all.

Of course, if she's a Wilding, that would explain after a fashion. They're all fanatics, but why Feyjak? They could knock off a lot of others more important. We got a tip she's hiding out on Ganymede. A place called the Spacerat's Roost. Know anything about it?"

The inspector whistled. "Not much. Enough to stay clear of the place. It's a dive in the Interplanetary Quarter, a damn tough hole. Mostly Plutonium prospectors and fungi hunters hang out there. We suspect it's mixed up in the illegal Moondrug traffic, but can't prove anything. I never send my boys into that quarter unless it's necessary, and then only in squads of four. Sure you don't want help?"

Heydrick grinned sourly. "I wouldn't want your boys to get their pretty uniforms dirty. Do you think you could make me look like a Plutonium prospector?"

"Can do—that all?"

"Draw me a map of the district. I'll need to know my way around."

"I'd rather draw it than show you. I wouldn't go there alone. Not at night. They don't like cops."

"Neither do I." Heydrick showed his teeth like an amiable wolf.

"If you're not back in two days, we'll come in after you."

"I'll be back."

The air in the Spacerat's Roost was thick with Fung-weed smoke. Heydrick mingled with the crowd inside the doorway and noticed men from every inhabited world in the Solar System. He spotted a vacant table and elbowed his way to it. A drug-soaked horror from Venus, obviously the bouncer, looked dubiously at the newcomer in his scuffed prospector's leather. Heydrick pounded on the table for service.

The waiter was a Jovian octopus man with five tentacles and three eyes. He came and hovered over the table, blinking sadly, as if life was a burden to him.

"What'll you have?"

"What've you got?"

The waiter waved a tentacle airily. "Anything you can name—Snow-grape Champagne from Mars, Deimos rice-nectar, Toad's-eye brandy and Banana-beer from Venus ..." he paused dramatically, leaned close and whispered, "even a bit of Blue Moonfoam from Callisto for special customers."

Heydrick winked. "I'm a special customer."

"You must have more money than sense," the waiter observed. "It'll be twenty vikdals, Martian."

Heydrick flicked a hundred vikdal platinum coin on the table. The octopus man uncoiled a tentacle and snatched it up, tested it for weight, then shambled off. He returned with a dusty bottle and the change. Heydrick let the change lie.

"Would you like to earn the rest of it?"

The octopus creature clucked somewhere within the unholy cavern which served him as mouth. "I'd kill anyone on Ganymede for half of that," he observed. "What'ya want me to do?"

Heydrick drew a deep breath. "You've a singer here who calls herself the *Red Leopard of Mars*. When does she go on?"

The waiter consulted a wrist-chron. "Anytime now. She's temperamental."

"When she's finished her turn, ask her to come to my table." The Jovian shrugged and moved off.

The houselights dimmed suddenly. A shower of colored lights played upon the raised stage. Soft nostalgic music poured from an unseen source. Soundlessly, a series of colored crystal screens slid back. At the back of the stage was a shadowy figure half-concealed by clouds of gossamer stuff blown wildly by concealed fans. Slowly, with infinite insolence, the figure moved to the point of the triangular stage. She stood motionless, waiting, while the babel of unearthly tongues died away in silence. The music grew louder. Veil by veil she flung off the filmy draperies until she stood revealed. Klathgar....

She wore the conventional garb of a woman of the ancient desert dwellers, jewelled copper breast-plates, a circlet of beaten bronze binding her wealth of red-violet hair, her eyes glittering like emerald fire; and the long divided skirt concealed little of her shapely body. Leashed, beside her, was the restless, slithering shadow of a red sand-leopard.

Against the wavering, eerie melody, and a patterned off-beat throb of tom-toms, she began to sing. Her voice was rich, throaty, and the song a poignant love song of the ancient desert people. For a moment Heydrick forgot where he was and who *she* was. The hopeless yearning and infinite tragedy of the music played unpleasantly with his soul-memories. The weird denizens of the Spacerat's Roost sat enthralled.

The song ended upon a note of earth-sick despair, a haunting melancholy for things that will never again be as they were, never, if the planets swing round a dead sun in an empty sky.

The singer bowed, half-contemptuously, to the storm of applause, then retired.

Heydrick drew the identification space-photo from his pocket and studied it. There was no doubt. Despite the heavy make-up, the features were the same. Ria Tarsen and Klathgar were the same.

In moments the girl was back. She had shed her glamor-costume and was nearly naked in the briefest of skirts, legs shimmering in painted stockings, high-breasts caught in a tight sheen of semi-translucent material. This time she sang a bawdy song, "If Asteroids were Asterisks," about a girl who went for a rocket-ride with an octopus man, and had to hitchhike home from the Moons of Jupiter.

The crowd went wild. The number finished with a rowdy burlesque dance which went considerably beyond the bounds of good taste, but was screamingly funny.

The girl ducked out the wings, and Heydrick nodded to the waiter. The octopus man winked one of his three eyes and vanished. He came back through the door to the dressing rooms, and the girl was with him. He pointed to Heydrick. Klathgar looked at him insolently. A puzzled frown wrinkled her face.

Lithe as a sand-leopard, she moved among the crowded tables, still clad in the gaudy costume of her last number.

Heydrick looked closely at her. Could this be the same girl who sang the love song so full of fiery passion that it was madness set to music? The uncanny warble of flutes and the triple throb of bone-drums still echoed in his ears. But this girl was tired; strain and unutterable weariness lurked behind her eyes.

"Why did you send for me?" she asked.

"I wanted to talk to you—is that so unusual?"

"Men always want to talk to me," she said, sneering. "I don't have to associate with the customers—not even those who can buy Moonfoam."

Heydrick noticed suddenly that the sand-leopard was with her. The animal's tail swished savagely back and forth. Its lips curled and a snarling burr of sound came from the ugly rows of teeth. It seemed like an echo of the girl's sneer. Klathgar put down one hand to stroke the beast's spade-shaped head. It rubbed against her in silent ecstasy.

"Perhaps I can change your mind," suggested Heydrick. "Won't you sit down?"

"You flatter yourself," she snapped. "I can hear what you have to say standing up."

"I wonder if you can," Heydrick mused aloud. "First, who are you?" The ghost of fear trembled behind her mask.

Klathgar laughed. "Ask anybody who I am. Klathgar. The Red Leopard."

Heydrick threw Ria Tarsen's dossier card on the table, face up. Klathgar glanced at it without a flicker of emotion.

"Is that supposed to mean something to me?" she asked contemptuously.

"It should—it's yours."

Her laugh was shrill. "At least you have a new approach. In either case, you're mistaken. What's your racket?"

"Heydrick, I.P.S. If you're not Ria Tarsen, who are you? May I see your ident-card?"

The girl was growing angry. "It's in my dressing room; I'll get it."

Heydrick was on his feet. "If you don't mind, I'll go with you."

"I do mind."

"I'll go anyway."

The girl shrugged and led the way among the crowded tables, the leopard padding silently beside her. Curious glances went with them. Suddenly Klathgar turned. "On second thought, I have it here," she said. She knelt quickly and unsnapped the leopard's leash. Heydrick's hand reached for his gun, but the girl was holding a card out to him. Even as he took it, he wondered if the gesture were a trick to occupy his gun hand.

One glance at the card was enough. "I hope you didn't pay too much for this," he told her. "It's a clumsy forgery."

Klathgar muttered a low word to the leopard, then slipped through the sliding door of plastic. A bundle of furred muscle launched itself at Heydrick. It was touch and go for a minute. Deadly talons raked through the leather tunic like razors. The man got a grip on the jewelled collar and twisted savagely. He wrenched the great cat away long enough to get out a paralysis gun and fire it. The drugged needle went into a soft spot behind one furred ear. Instantly the beast let go and crumpled.

Heydrick leaped for the door. Someone tried to trip him, but he got through and slammed the plastic door shut.

Cutting down the intensity of his blaster, he ran the blunt muzzle up and down the joint where the heavy slab of plastic fit, sealing it tightly as the plastic flowed and fused. "That should hold them," he thought. Something crashed against the door.

In the dim passageway, Heydrick could see several doors, all shut. Which door?

He tried three, then saw one marked with a glittering star. It was locked, but he put his shoulder against it and shoved violently. The thin screen buckled.

The girl was rummaging in a drawer. She turned and lunged at him with an ornamental dagger. Heydrick wrenched it away from her.

"Nice try, Ria."

She leaped on him, kicking and scratching. Locked together they crashed into the mirror. All three went down in a smash of glass. The girl lay still.

Heydrick took a needle from the paralysis gun and scratched her lightly. Her breathing steadied and she lay relaxed, while he opened the window and looked out. Below him, bathed in eerie Jupiter-light, lay the rooftops of the city. He could just make it to the next roof. Ria was lighter than she looked.

At security police headquarters, Heydrick sat back for a quiet smoke. He had changed back into the crisp silvery grey of the Space Patrol. The inspector was in an official mood. He had his shoes on.

"What's the quickest transportation back to Mars?"

The inspector grinned. "Anxious to get her off your hands, eh? I don't blame you. The Martian Express is the quickest—you can get it at City

1. It doesn't stop, of course, but they pick up ore-lighters as they go past Ganymede."

"How can I get to City 1?"

"I'll lend you a patrol flier. They're all old crates, rocket drive. If it gets you there, you can leave it; we'll pick it up. If not, maybe we'll get some decent equipment."

Heydrick walked down the dim passageway to the cell in which he had deposited Ria Tarsen. She glowered at him.

"Did you kill my leopard?"

"He's all right. Be stiff a couple of days, that's all. I used the paralysis gun. How d'you feel."

The girl did not answer. Heydrick went on. "I'm sorry, Ria. I'll have to take you back now." He unlocked the cell, and the girl strode into the corridor. She was still arrogant and glared at him with cold insolence.

"You must feel proud of yourself," she said icily. "You'll never get me back to Mars."

"I thought of that." He took a metal bracelet from his pocket. "Try this on for size."

"That's a funny handcuff; it's not chained to anything," she said as he clasped it on her wrist.

"Try running away," he suggested. Ria darted down the corridor, then stopped as if she had run smack into a dur-steel wall.

"Magnetic," he explained. "Can be set for distances up to fifty feet. Once that's on you, and the mate to it's on me, we're linked together to the end of the trail. It's sealed with a coded beam of light. I don't have the combination. I just don't want you to try anything silly, that's all."

"I'll kill you for this," Ria promised, her green eyes glowing with ugly light.

"Seems you've killed one man too many now," Heydrick commented. "Even if you were lucky enough to kill me, we'd still be linked together; you couldn't escape with a corpse."

"I didn't kill Feyjak 9," she shrieked. "I didn't kill him. It was an accident. I don't know anything about it."

Heydrick looked at her soberly. "I don't believe you, Ria. And, if I did, it wouldn't matter. You were tried and sentenced. I'm sorry for you, but it's my job to take you back to the—to your punishment."

"I won't go back to the disintegrators," Ria stated, her face pale but tearless. "You'll never get me there alive."

In the antiquated patrol flier, Heydrick set the auto-pilot for City 1. The girl was sleeping quietly under the effects of the paralysis drug. Heydrick went back to the galley and opened a can of hot coffee. A sudden tug at the metal circlet on his wrist sent him racing to the controls.

It was too late. The girl held a heavy bar of dur-steel ready to crash it down on the maze of keys and switch-bars. The bar descended in a glittering crescent. Blue flame shot through the tiny cabin. Rocket jets fused and exploded at the tail of the rocket-flier.

The shock knocked Heydrick to his knees. He scrambled to the control board and reached for the girl. In one movement, she turned and struck at him with the bar. It missed his head, but a numbing jar went through his shoulder. A clip on the jaw sent her reeling.

Frantically Heydrick worked at the wrecked controls, splicing burnt wires, bending keys back to position. Sick nausea clawed at his insides. The ship was going down in a free fall, spinning. The thin atmosphere of Ganymede went round the hull with a crescendo, whistling scream. A jagged wilderness of saw-toothed rock and volcanic ash whirled up at the flier.

The slight gravity of Ganymede was bad enough, but if they struck at full rocket velocity, the hull would crumple like an eggshell. With a length of wire, Heydrick burned his fingers shorting the switches to the forward tubes. It was too late to do much. If he could only slow the fall.

A series of explosions forward jarred through the ship. Deceleration flung Heydrick on top of the girl.

The flier buried her nose in soft ash and skidded thirty yards in a choking shower. A sharp needle of jagged rock reached up through the dust to catch her. With a shriek of riven metal the flier rose on end. The fused-quartz port-holes bulged and gave way.

Supercharged air whistled out of the cabin. As the artificially heavy air blew itself out, Heydrick felt his head swell as if it were going to explode. His eyes seemed to be squeezing out of his head. Dazed, he groped to the locker and got out the space-suits. The cold bit into him like needles of ice till he struggled into his suit. He set his atmosphere control, then fought his way through the shattered wreckage to Ria. She was in no condition to resist as he forced the bulky space-suit on her. He set the controls on her suit, then talked into his microphone.

"You are a problem child," he said. "How'd you manage it?"

Ria was sick and dizzy. She staggered on her feet. "I had some benzedrine—stole it from the emergency kit. Your paralysis needle barely scratched me anyhow."

She fell weakly against the bulkhead. Heydrick seized her and dragged her through the riven shell of the control room into the shelter of a gaunt outcropping.

"The forward rockets are building up. They'll go any minute."

A bellowing geyser of dust-shrouded flame roared up. Flying metal clattered brutally on their shelter.

"Just in time," he said. Ria lay on the ground, retching weakly. "Well, the security boys get a new ship. They'll be happy. From here on, we walk. I hope you're satisfied."

The upper limb of an immense crescent rose above the horizon. Jupiter. Its sombre light revealed a savage wasteland of barren rock and volcanic ash.

"Come on, Babe. You should enjoy this. It's thirty miles, and the walking's bad. But we like it that way, don't we?"

Sulkily, Ria got to her feet and followed him.

The Martian Express Liner, *Phobos*, went into full gear with a velocity of 89 Martian gravities. After detouring the dangerous asteroid belt, the ship nosed down in a long curving glide to intercept the orbit of Mars. Far ahead was a blurred crescent of red, glowing with soft radiance against a star-sprinkled void. Lee Heydrick watched the planet swing slowly across the field of the glass. A deep unrest troubled him, but he refused to face the mask it might wear and tried to force it out of his mind.

"We should be there in fourteen hours," the co-pilot said.

"That'll be a relief. This is one job I don't like."

The pilot glanced at them sourly. "I thought you were through with the service," he shot at Heydrick.

"I am—it's my last job. I can't live on any of the inner planets after being exposed to the zero-rays of outer space. It takes six months for a resignation to go through in the Space Patrol. My time is up in two weeks and four days. After that, I'll have to stick to the places outside the asteroid belt or resign myself to a very brief life—18 months, at the outside."

"Too bad. What're you going to do?"

"I don't know. Maybe settle on one of the Moons of Saturn. They aren't too crowded. I'll be glad to be free again. Silly, isn't it—when you think of the way I used to look forward to being in Space Patrol! My folks were refugees from earth—lived in the icy marshes near the northern ice-cap of Mars. I ran away from home to go to Canal City 9 and study for the Patrol. My grades were good enough to impress Tyko. He took me into his home. My folks were proud of me. They're all dead now; Tyko's all I have left. I'll miss the old buzzard."

The co-pilot grunted. "What are you kicking about? I wish somebody'd handcuff me to a kitten like that one of yours. She looks hotter than a rocket tube. If you get tired of your work, I'll take over and spell you awhile."

Heydrick grinned with embarrassment. "You might regret it. She's tried to kill me twice already. She's full of ideas."

"I hope she knocks you off—you can will her to me."

The alarms through the space cruiser began to shrill in great bellows of sound. Heydrick ran along the passageway and tried the door of the stateroom where he had locked his prisoner. It was still locked. He used the key, but something heavy was jammed against the door. He drew his blaster gun and cut down the intensity. The door glowed cherry red, then flowed together. It gave as he crashed against it.

Ria was posed dramatically, metal stool in hand, in the act of trying to smash the port-cover. The fused-quartz pane was already spiderwebbed, and air sucked out in a rising whine. Ria changed her mind and flung the stool at Heydrick. He lunged under it and caught her round the waist. In one movement, he flung her over his shoulder and whirled back out to the passage. Dropping her in a heap, he clawed shut the insulated emergency door and spun the wing-nuts. Waves of cold licked his eyelashes and his fingers stung with frost before he got the job done.

The girl's green eyes watched him warily, as a cat's might.

"I'm sorry you made it," she spat at him viciously. "I hate you—hate you!"

Heydrick spun the dials on the handcuffs. "Okay, kid, if you want to play rough, you'll sit out the rest of the trip on my lap. The interval is two feet, as of now."

"I hope you can take it." Then she snapped. Tears burst out. She raged and screamed and kicked, laughed and cried and choked at the same time. Heydrick slapped her out of it. She huddled on the floor, sobbing weakly.

The co-pilot came along the passageway. "Oh, it's your pet? We thought it might be."

"Still want to trade jobs?"

"It might be fun to spank her, but I'll skip it. I've news for you. We can't land in City 4—trouble of some kind—sounds like a good row."

"Do you know what's wrong?"

"They didn't say. Orders are to take the ship on the Desert City 12. You two can go down in the lighters with the freight." The co-pilot patted Ria on the shoulder—she cringed away from him. "Tough luck," he said gently. "Too bad you're stuck with Bighead here. If you were dealing with me, we'd go off to some empty asteroid and camp out for the rest of your life."

Brooding over the immensity of the plain below was Canal City 4. Covering the entire city like a tremendous bubble was the iridescent dome of fused-quartz. The tiny fleet of ore-lighters nosed through the valves of airlock after airlock and headed across town toward the sprawling terraces of the freight docks. Like a chain of brightly silvered pumpkin seeds, the clumsy craft wound in and out among the towers of the 7th level, down to the freight docks.

Heydrick took his prisoner through the airlock in the freight terminal to condition her and himself for street-level atmosphere, then went out on the huge platform again.

Pausing only long enough to ask a robot attendant for information, Heydrick pushed the button to stop a descending elevator.

"Labor trouble—the workers are picketing—riots have broken out at street level," droned the mechanical voice of the robot.

A crowded car stopped, signalling raucously. Heydrick showed his badge to the robot pilot. "Street level," he said crisply. "Space Patrol priority." The robot grunted. "We have orders not to stop unless it's vitally necessary."

"It's necessary."

Jumbles of neo-plastic architecture, rising tier on tier above the series of terraces on which the city was built, whirled upward past the descending car.

On the street level, all was bustle and confusion. A polyglot crowd composed of every human and near human species in the universe jammed the streets. Stares followed the I.P.S. uniform as Heydrick pushed out of the elevator. A few people gave nods of respect, but in most faces burned a sullen hatred and resentment.

Ria followed him in stolid silence as the handcuffs tugged at her. The knots of angry people came suddenly in focus and she had a moment's desperate inspiration.

She jerked back heavily on the cuffs and began to scream.

Heydrick was caught off guard and spun sharply about.

"Help me, somebody," Ria cried wildly. "The cops are taking me in. I haven't done anything."

The mob clotted around the pair, snarling angrily.

Heydrick reached for his gun, just as somebody threw a spanner. He dodged, heard Ria's voice shout a welcome, "Thorsan," and that was all. A sharp jab in his cheek as the paralysis needle went home was the last he knew. Darkness rushed over him in a smothering cloud.

Someone kept slapping him. He felt as if he were trying to swim in thick syrup. The light on the desk shone blindingly in his eyes. He got his hand up to shield his eyes, then they struck it down. He blinked sharply awake.

Behind the desk sat a handsome man. Pale blue eyes that probed deeply, plump cheeks, thick blonde eyebrows, muscular shoulders. Heydrick had seen him before. Where? Oh, yes—the pieces clicked together. The Feyjak investigation. The man had testified against Ria Tarsen, reluctantly, the Visiphone News had commented. He had been Feyjak's assistant, Ria's friend.

Thorsan drummed the desk with his fingers. "Heydrick, you've given us a lot of trouble. You probably want to know where you are. You're in the underground galleries below Level 1. We have our headquarters here. I am the head man of the Wildings."

Heydrick's brain spun. He fought back the whirl and tried to think calmly.

Below the lowest inhabited level of Canal City 4 were endless mazes of caverns, galleries and abandoned mine-shafts.

Rumor said that bands of outlaws roamed among the savages, second and third generations of the outcast rebels who long-ago had been driven to the refuge of the city's ratholes. Banded together by their common hatreds, these outlaws had built up a strong organization known as the Wildings. There was some talk that numbers of them had infiltrated the City's government; men of dangerous ability, infinite cunning, and vicious philosophy, whose sole aim was the overthrow of the Government of Scientists.

Heydrick's heart turned suddenly to ashes as he realized that Ria Tarsen must have been a Wilding. Surely no group would have gone to the trouble of instigating riots merely to rescue an outsider, however innocent. It was all clear now, painfully clear.

Thorsan must have divined the nature of Heydrick's thoughts. He laughed harshly, then turned to a subordinate.

"They're no use to us, either of them. The girl didn't know as much as I thought she did. Now they both know too much. We'll have to get rid of them. Put him in the cell with her while I figure out what to do with them."

Hands reached out of the darkness and dragged Heydrick roughly to his feet. He was thrust along a winding gallery that he realized must be part of an old mine. They must have given him a full dose with the paralysis needle. He kept stumbling, and his legs moved stiffly.

The group came to a halt before an old wooden-plank door. The room inside was damp, and smelled mouldy. It was evidently a chamber cut in the rock for storage of explosives. His captors thrust him inside. He bounced off a wall and fell heavily. The door bumped shut and a sound like a bar dropping in place came muffled through the planks.

"Well, tough guy, how do *you* like being pushed around?" A familiar voice came out of darkness.

"Who is it?" he asked needlessly.

"It's not your Aunt Sophie," the voice said acidly. "*You* should kick. You have better company than I have."

The two sat in moody silence for a while. "Are you all right?" the girl asked finally.

"Still stiff," he answered. "You should know what that's like."

"I do. You and your toy handcuffs. They only wanted me; Thorsan thought I knew he killed Feyjak. He was afraid I might give him away. They had to drag you along on account of your silly handcuffs. If you hadn't split my lip, I could laugh at you. They're going to kill us, you know."

"Yes, I heard him say that."

"What are we going to do? Any ideas?"

"Not so far. How about you?"

"Nothing definite. I still have the benzedrine tablets I swiped. They didn't find 'em when they searched me. I'll split with you. If we take it before they come for us, we may get a chance to make a break. It'll counteract the paralysis drug if they're counting on that to make us dead pigeons while they haul us around."

Her hand found his in the dark and thrust six pellets into his open palm. Her fingers were wet and sticky.

"You're bleeding."

"It's nothing serious. That bracelet of yours cut my arm when they chiselled it off."

"I'm sorry about everything, Ria—"

"Skip it," she said harshly. "Of course you're sorry. Now shut up. I hate post-mortems. Besides, I think they're coming. Better get your benzedrine down."

There was sound of the bar being withdrawn. A heavy foot kicked the door open. A man with a twisted face held the light and the gun while two others approached warily and jabbed needles into the captives. Coarse hands jerked them to their feet, and the two were dragged outside, feigning limpness.

"Now," said Ria. She thrust out her foot. The man with the gun tripped and went sprawling on the floor. Heydrick swung with all he had at the darkness where he remembered a chin and felt bone shatter beneath his fist. Then he was tangled in a savage knot with the third man, rolling and threshing about in deadly fury.

Ria was not idle. She salvaged the light, switched the radilume back on, and hunted for the dropped gun. In a matter of seconds, she brought the butt down on an exposed skull. The thug let go and sank to the floor.

Heydrick dusted himself off.

"I ought to let you have it, too," Ria mumbled, "but I always was a softy. Come on, sucker."

"Which way?"

"I think they brought me that way," the girl said slowly. "Let's try the other. Heaven knows where it leads."

Heydrick took the gun from her and thrust it through his belt. They struck off down the tunnel, taking forks at random, but going as cautiously as they could.

Luck was against them. They came suddenly round a turn and into a chamber full of Wildings. It was the room where Heydrick had been questioned by Thorsan. The man still sat at the desk. Heydrick drew the gun and pressed its trigger as Thorsan dived for a doorway. The desk glowed, then exploded. The room was choked with dust.

Heydrick remembered a nightmarish pursuit, running down a series of criss-cross galleries with endless side passages. The gallery ended abruptly. An open mine-shaft barred their way.

It was a double shaft, with space for two elevators, but neither lift was on their level. Sounds of pursuit came from the gallery behind them.

Heydrick leaned over and looked down the shaft. A floor below was the open-platform lift.

"Jump for the cable," he ordered. "Try to slide down it."

"You first," she said. "I'm a sissy." Heydrick jumped and his stomach wrenched with nausea. Then the cable was burning through his hands. His feet stung as they came down solidly on the metal flooring. The girl was right behind him. He found the control lever and jammed it all the way over.

The car dropped under them with sickening speed.

A blaster beam flamed briefly above them, and the discharge set a chorus of echoes bouncing back and forth in the old mine-shaft.

"Hang tight," he shouted. "I don't know how far down this shaft goes. If we hit bottom at this speed, we'll flatten out like saucers."

A mushroom of brilliant light expanded above them. The car jerked and grated on the rock walls, then went down in a free fall, the cable trailing slack above them.

Down the shaft hurtled the old lift, air whistling eerily round its edges.

"They've blasted the cable!" Heydrick cried. "Now we are in for it." He leaped to the brake lever and tugged at it. The bar was rusted fast. Ria tried to help. With their combined weight and effort, the bar gave a little. Inch by inch, it moved. The clamps started taking hold of the side walls and a shriek of protest came from rock and metal. The elevator slowed slightly. Too late.

With a grinding rasp of smashed metal, it struck. Ria was hurled clear, but Heydrick was trapped.

The metal cable came down, coiling and snapping like a whip. A stiff spiral of it covered Heydrick, pinning him fast to the floor. He wiped a smear of blood from his face and tried vainly to lift the heavy strands. They refused to budge.

Ria knelt beside him and tried to shift the coils, but it was no use.

"You'd better go," he said roughly. "They'll be down as soon as they can get to the other elevator ... to make sure of us."

Ria glared at him. "It's my maternal instinct," she said. "I can't leave you."

"You wanted a chance to escape. This is it."

Ria seized the broken brake lever and pried up part of the strands. Heydrick worked himself part way out, but the weight was too much for her strength. The bar twisted out of her hands. Down came the full weight again. Heydrick cried out in agony. She moved the bar and lifted again. This time, he crawled free.

Leaning on her, he was able to stand and walk along the old gallery, but it was a slow business. Deadly slow.

Behind them, they could hear the whine of a descending lift. "They're coming," he said. Crouching against an angle of the tunnel, they waited. It was useless to run. Heydrick cut the switch of his radilume and braced the blaster against cold stone. He felt better with the trigger nestling against his trembling finger.

The Wildings came cautiously, but they needed light to move at all.

Light splashed off the rock around the corner. Shadowy figures moved behind the light. Heydrick pressed the trigger, and a pale beam flicked the darkness. In the close confinement of the tunnel, the shattering blast stunned their brains.

The explosion stopped some of the pursuit, but a scuff of boots on rough rock warned Heydrick. Needles from paralysis guns snicked nastily from the naked rocks beside them. He and the girl turned and fled head-long through the darkness. Pain forgotten, he thrust Ria ahead of him, and pried up part of the strands. Heydrick followed, stumbling and swearing.

In the darkness ahead, he heard Ria cry out. Unable to stop, he too col-lided with what seemed to be a solid wall of metal. Heydrick flicked the radilume switch. Light flooded an ore depot, with rusting electric cars.

"Ore cars," he gasped. "Get in." He boosted the girl up and scrambled after her. Heydrick fumbled for the switch, found it. The car leaped ahead as a blaster beam licked the rails behind them. With shaking hands, Hey-drick re-primed his blaster and fired wildly at the darkness behind them. Shadows danced. It seemed seconds before the blasts went off. Two in rapid succession.

Another car leaped from the dust cloud behind. It was pursuing them on the parallel tracks.

A blaster beam grazed the back wall of the ore-car. It was gone with a flash and a roar. The shock flattened Heydrick and the girl against the front wall. Heydrick re-primed his gun, but it was impossible to aim. The tracks went into a black maw and went up in a steeply climbing spiral. Flanges screamed wildly as the wheels bit into the curves. Up. Up. Up. The miles raced backward in a dizzy flow of darkness lit by faint reflec-tions from the radilume.

Suddenly the track levelled off on a straightaway. Heydrick peered ahead. Heaven alone knew where the tunnel led or how far the tracks were good. The car was going like a runaway rocket.

Then they were out in the open, in daylight. The tracks came out of a tunnel-mouth on the banks of the dry canal.

The hurtling ore-car was half way across the bridge before Heydrick knew they were heading for the city.

Out of the tunnel-mouth across the canal shot the other ore-car. Both cars raced toward the city.

Ten miles. Five. Three. One.

Weird lights flickered on the tremendous dome ahead, as if some infernal carnival was being held within the city.

Up a steep ramp to the airlock shot the cars. Seconds now. The airlock was closed.

A gate of metal and plastic loomed close. Glass, plastic, metal and quartz vanished in a thunderous melee of sound. The first lock. The city's automatic wall-magnets clawed at the racing car. It slowed rapidly. The deceleration pinned both of them flat against the front wall of the car. It went through the second gate like a knife through dough. The jar was agony.

The car rolled up to a dock and stopped.

Heydrick was out of the car and racing for a visiphone as a wobbling wheel came loose and romped down the track, smashing sheds to metal splinters.

"Get Tyko," he bellowed.

"Sorry," a robot said tonelessly. "No calls are going through till the end of the emergency."

Heydrick swore wildly. He and Ria ran through the building and out onto the huge terrace in front. The vast bowl of the city was in tumult. Fires were raging on all the lower levels, and several of the towers of the 7th level had crashed down in ruins. Mobs roared through the streets, killing, burning, and looting. It was revolution. Security police, trying to stem the outbreak, were caught in the maelstroms, overwhelmed, and submerged. The lower levels had gone mad with hate. Wildings were everywhere, organizing, leading, destroying.

Heydrick commandeered an empty flier, got Ria aboard and set the automatic pilot for Tyko's tower in West 21.

In Tyko's tower, the old man stood watching the end of the grim spectacle in the streets below. Walls of white fire moved out in ever-widening circles from the experimental domes, moved through the city, quieting the mobs, herding them back to their homes. Dead lay in windrows.

A bell rang behind him. He turned. "Oh, come in," he said. It was Thorsan, Feyjak's assistant.

"It's almost over," Tyko told him. "Order is being restored now. After this, we'll keep the Blues in power and give the people a government they can like. It's a sad thing, to govern people. Herding them about like animals. Men should be free. I'm an anarchist myself ... out of hours."

"How about my people?" Thorsan asked, an odd expression on his face.

"Your people? Oh, the Red Scientists. Don't worry. We knew this revolt was coming, even if you Reds didn't. We've had our eye on the Wildings for some time. You Reds are safe enough. When order is restored, perhaps a joint government...."

Tyko stopped. He was looking into the muzzle of a blaster.

"I don't understand," he quavered.

"My people are the Wildings. We don't want any of your kind of governments," Thorsan said slowly. "With you out of the way, nothing can stop the revolution. I regret the necessity."

From the open doorway, Heydrick fired. The paralysis needle bit deep in Thorsan's neck. He crumpled silently.

Heydrick and Ria stood before Tyko.

"I see you've completed your mission," the old man said. He frowned as Heydrick put his arm around Ria.

Heydrick laughed. "When Thorsan comes out of it, give him scopolamine. He'll tell you who did kill Feyjak."

"I suppose you want my blessing? You have it."

"How's your war coming?"

"It's over by now. Nasty business, government. What are you going to do?"

Heydrick and Ria looked at each other.

"I think we'll find an empty asteroid and camp out for a while. The universe is getting too crowded. I'm glad she was innocent, Tyko. I could never have brought her in ... for any reason."

"I wish I were young enough to go with you," Tyko sighed. "Not on your honeymoon, of course. I guess you won't be coming back. This is goodbye, then? Is there anything I can do for you?"

Heydrick started to reply but Ria cut in. "Yes, there is. I want another pair of those magnetic handcuffs."

Heydrick shrugged. "She has the maternal instincts of a buzz-saw."

THE END

EYE COLLECTOR SEARCH-A-WORD

Fill in the blanks and find the words!

```
O J M A F I L W D L T L Q L Q M F R Y Q I
C Q T W Z Z T T C N C D A C I K B E T H K
T M I U I K J X D R A R B G Y C E W T P H
G Q S M Q W R X R P A S W L E S C Z L B Q
T S D B S T A C U Q D C U K O L L J B V G
C A P T A I N C R U N C H O R G A R X K V
C J O J Q Y U G M D K V O E H Q N R C T O
M S N F P S Q L H M U U Y D L T Z K A E D
I H K N V S G D V S L L K C Y O E Y N P K
T A J Z V T X N I H D Z L L C Q E N O S A
R G R N Y P G E H R W E N X G Y S S O J T
T J H Y S M L Y F Y H E M T S V Y D S Y L
L L Q J H O U T Q D C B A X F B H B G F V
T F T Y D T E V P K D E L C V I B Y P F Z
H M P B A K H B L C P Q T G J F F M T B Y
Z F J W V V O A H N O I T A E L C U N E A
Z J N U L W C E I O Q W V E S H P X F Y H
S E N A Z E T A A V N E J O D L C J Z E S
T P N Y V R G Y N Y N E D Z V M E X E O E
J B C I Q E P H W F B R R T N E M E S A B
O R M C U U M J H J R U D S Y B S Q M R I
```

1. D.R. ate two bowls of _______ _____ cereal.
2. In the end, Dylan offered Teri ___ _____ dollars for her services.
3. ______ necklace.
4. ______ and _____ are the two victims Dylan did not write about.
5. _________ spoon.
6. Rebecca was a _______ for Long, Peeler, and Ingle.
7. The floor where Dylan kept his eye collection. ________
8. How old was D.R. when he killed the squirrel? ___
9. The drink Dylan ordered the night he met Rebecca. ______

THANKS FOR JOINING THE ADVENTURES!

FOR NEXT ISSUES AND MORE VISIT:
www.OffBeatReads.com